The Roots of Elvis

Julian Riley

The Roots of Elvis

All pictures and Stories are personal property of the author and/or Mackey Hargett.

Published by arrangement with the author.

Copyright © 2010 by Julian C. Riley

All rights reserved.

This book, or parts thereof may not be reproduced in any form without the express written consent from the author. The scanning and distribution of this book via any means without the permission of the publisher is illegal and punishable by law.

Your support of author's rights is appreciated.

ISBN 978-1-4507-1808-0

Printed by Paw Pad Printing
3665 South Perkins Rd.
Suite #9
Memphis, TN 38118
Printed in United States of America

Introduction	5
Welcome To My World	11
Pocket Full of Rainbows	32
For The Good Times	36
Blue Eyed Handsome Man	58
Heartbreak Hotel	65
Loving You	70
Trying To Get To You	74
So Close Yet So Far	76
The Green, Green Grass of Home	82
Little Sister	103
I'm Movin' On	111
A Mess of Blues	124
Jailhouse Rock	140
That's Alright Mama	161
Memories	163
Conclusions	202

Introduction

Native Mississippians Julian Riley and Rachel Ann Harden have spent the last four years researching the genealogical roots of Elvis Presley. Riley, a local historian and genealogist, and Harden, an avid Elvis fan, have joined forces to create a website loaded with information about all sides of Elvis's family. These two researchers are the foremost authorities concerning the complete Elvis Presley family tree. The site contains extensive research of the Presley, Hood, Smith, and Mansell family lines. Over 15,000 names and over 2,000 pictures and documents are on-line. The web site is www.rootsofelvispresley.com.

The purpose of this research is not to sensationalize people or events. The purpose is to record an extensive family tree, correct some misinformation concerning past research, and give readers a better appreciation of the lives of rural families in Mississippi after the War for Southern Independence. The War had left Mississippi and other Southern States devastated economically. Surviving day to day was particularly hard for Southern women. Thousands of young men had been killed, maimed, or mentally scarred by the War. There were few young men available for young women to marry. Often women married men much older than themselves. There were no social programs for women to rely on such as minimum wage, welfare, food stamps, social security, or Medicare. People living at that time should not be judged by today's standards.

You will learn about the lives of two sisters, Rosella and

The Roots of Elvis

Rosalinda Presley. They were abandoned by their father, their mother died when they were very young, and they lived for over twenty years down a dirt road in rural Itawamba County with their grandmother. Though neither woman was educated or ever married, they survived all the hard times after the war, and together they raised fourteen children. It is from the lineage of Rosella Presley that Elvis would be born.

One of the many discoveries is that the roots of Elvis Presley's family could not be deeper anywhere on earth, than in the red hills of Itawamba County, Mississippi. Rosella, her sister, Rosalinda, Jesse Dee Presley, Vernon Presley, and Noah Presley along with Minnie Mae Hood were all born outside of Fulton in Itawamba County. Itawamba County is overflowing with the history of these large families, and the early history of Northeast Mississippi. Elvis Presley was born just west of the Itawamba County line, in East Tupelo, Lee County, Mississippi.

Another intriguing discovery was the man who fathered Jesse Dee Presley; the great grandfather of Elvis Presley. Researchers of the Presley family have speculated about the father of Jesse Dee Presley for many years. Now, we believe the true father has been documented, and he was also born in Itawamba County.

The research into the many lines of this Southern family led in directions that could not have been imagined at the beginning of the project. Many local homes, courthouses, libraries, and cemeteries were visited. Many surviving family members were interviewed and many shared their records and pictures with us. Only someone known and trusted by these families would have had access to these records. Some of the information we needed was not available, and some of the stories were confusing. Some of the courthouses have burned and some of the graves are unmarked. Not all of the questions have been answered, and any new information, pictures, or comments concerning the Roots of Elvis Presley would be welcome. This is intended to be a thorough, ongoing project and it will be kept continually updated. This is the first book about the Presley family that has been researched and written by someone who has family buried in the same cemeteries as Elvis, who has lived in the same areas of Tupelo as Elvis and attended the same school as Elvis, and who is familiar with the local area and its history.

    Few people are recognized worldwide by their first name only. A small town country boy from Northeast Mississippi happens to be one, who, for the last 50 years has been instantly recognizable all over the world by his first name only. Interest in Elvis Presley has grown every year since he rocked onto the public stage with his first recording. Many books have been written about Elvis, and much research has been done into every area of his life. The fact that there could still be something interesting to discover about Elvis Presley might come as a surprise to some. Many people have conducted research into the family tree of Elvis Presley. Much of the work is good, some of it is bad, many errors have been made, and too much has been left unanswered. Our intention is to fill in the pieces of the puzzle, answer the questions, and correct the errors that we find. We hope to explain what happened without making any judgments or sensationalizing any events or people.

The Roots of Elvis

The story of Elvis Presley's roots is a story of hardships, heartbreak, and survival of rural Mississippi people. We have attempted to do as complete a research into the roots of Elvis as can be achieved. We have an advantage in that by living in Lee County, Mississippi, we are close to much of the information that needs to be researched. It would be difficult to do this research from any other location. We have a disadvantage in that many of the people with firsthand knowledge have died. Without the research and interviews done by others, the family tree that we have created would not have been possible. In some cases, we will refer to interviews that were conducted by other researchers many years ago. The family bibles, the marriage records at many courthouses, the cemetery records accumulated by local historic societies, the census records taken by the various governments, the family trees and old pictures saved by interested family members, and the local libraries have made this work possible. Many of the questions do not have a provable answer. If there is no provable answer, we will tell what we believe to be the most reasonable, simple, and realistic answer. We have tried to only use some form of public record, and when none can be found we will state that we could not find it. New uncovered information has proved some of the earlier research to be wrong about some of the stories. Many people have invited us into their homes and made us feel welcome. This would be expected of the people of Mississippi. We would like to thank all the many people who have been a tremendous help in this project. We would like to thank you very much for your interest in our research.

The Roots of Elvis

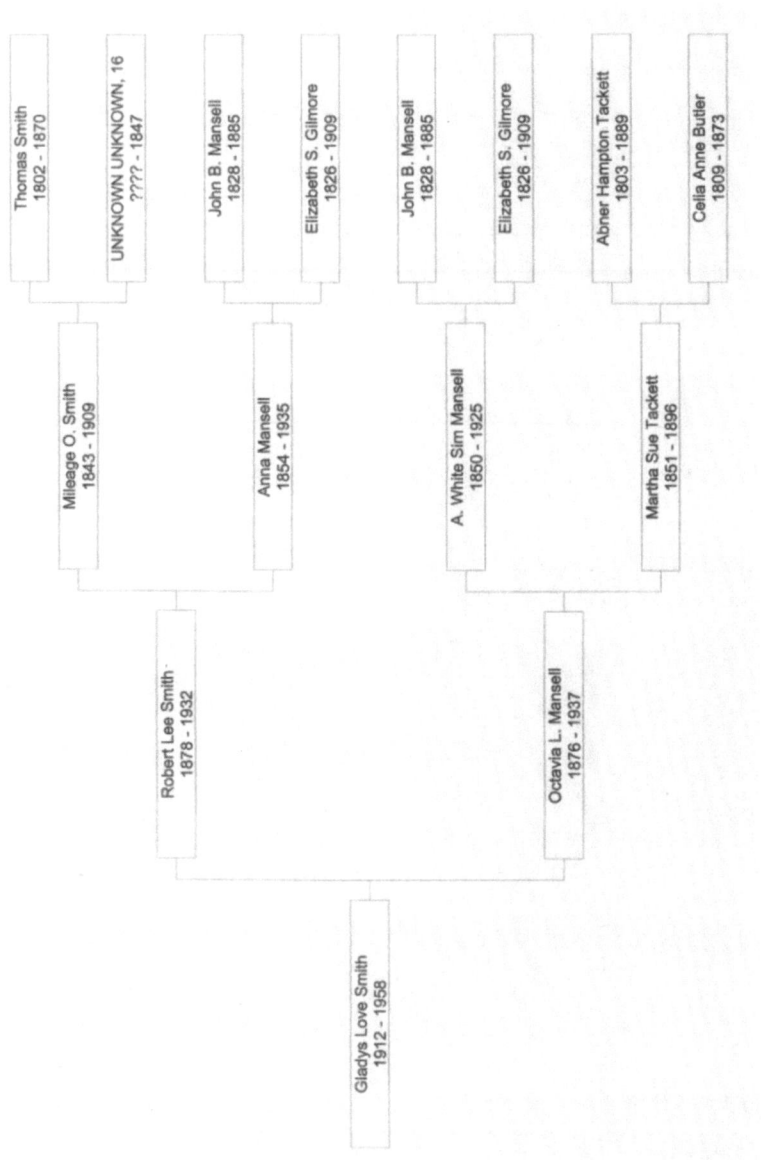

Family Tree Of Gladys Smith Presley

The Roots of Elvis

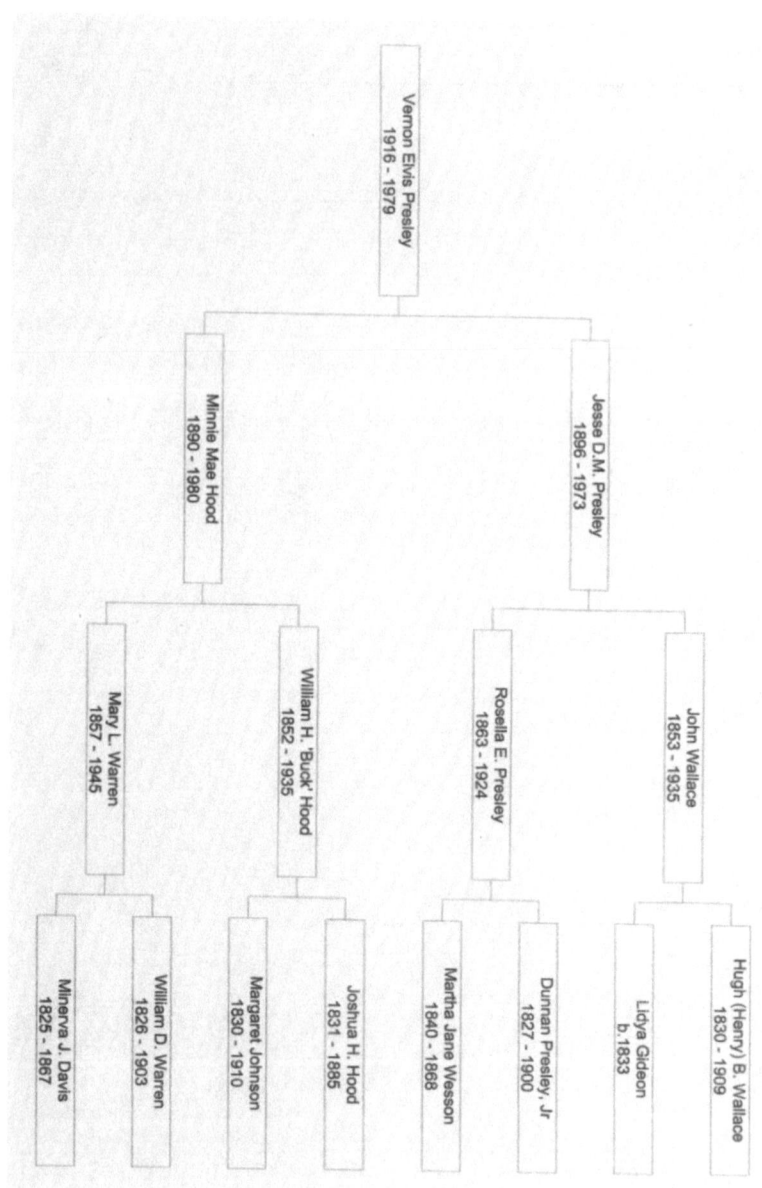

Family Tree Of Vernon Elvis Presley

Welcome To My World

    I have had an interest in history most all of my life. When I was five years old at my grandparent's home at Richmond, Lee County, Mississippi, my aunt came in from the cotton field with an Indian arrowhead she had found. Something about holding that ancient arrowhead in my small hand, created an interest in history that, at times, has been all consuming of my time and efforts. On each visit to the Richmond area, I would look in the fields and around my grandparent's house for Indian artifacts. Over the next 50 years, I accumulated one of the largest collections of Indian artifacts in the state of Mississippi. In 1980, I coauthored, with friends, Buddy Palmer and Steve Cook, a research paper on the locations of the historic Chickasaw Indian villages. The locations and names of these ancient Chickasaw villages had never been documented. Historians for the Chickasaw Nation have used this work as the basis of researching and recording the history of their people while they lived in Northeast Mississippi.

    My schoolteacher in fourth and fifth grade at Verona Elementary School, Miss Winnie Wharton, helped inspire an interest in history that is one of the reasons I am involved in writing this book. She was able to help a young boy who was not a good student, develop into a student with a strong desire to achieve. In 1964, when I was in school at Mississippi State University, I researched and wrote a term paper on the history of the Old Town of Richmond, Mississippi. Richmond was founded in the early 1840's; it is one of the oldest towns in what is now Lee County, Mississippi. Many of the founding families of Verona and Tupelo first settled in Richmond, Mississippi. In 1964, I could not possibly have known about the many connections of Richmond, Mississippi to the Elvis Presley story.

My mother's family has always attended church at Andrews Chapel, a small wooden country church about 2 miles north of Richmond and three miles south of Mooreville, in Lee County. This is the first church that I can remember attending. When me my mother and my brother, Larry, would visit my maternal grandparents at Richmond, we would attend Sunday school and church, at the same church many of Elvis Presley's family had attended. My mother would take peanut butter, crackers, and a jar of water for my brother and me to eat when we would get restless. There would be all day singings and dinner on the ground, with many walks through the old cemetery. Little did I know that I was walking around the tombstones of many of Elvis Presley's family?

Tombstone Of Effie Smith, Sister Of Gladys Smith

In 2002, while researching my family tree at the Andrews Chapel Cemetery, I found the small concrete tombstone of a child named Effie Smith. Effie was the daughter of Robert Lee and Doll Mansell Smith. She was Gladys Smith's sister, and Elvis Presley's aunt, buried within 20 feet of my grandparents, James Thomas and Mittie Smith Westmoreland. Can you imagine my excitement at finding this tombstone of Elvis Presley's aunt? At that time, I knew nothing about the Richmond, Mississippi, Hussey Farm, and Andrews Chapel connection to the Elvis Presley family tree. This would come a few years later.

I was born in Tupelo, Mississippi in December 1942. We lived on South Spring Street in the same Mill Town area of

South Tupelo where Gladys and Elvis had lived from 1938 until the summer of 1943. Gladys and Elvis lost their house on Old Saltillo Road in East Tupelo when Vernon was sentenced to Parchman prison. Gladys and Elvis lived at several different places in East Tupelo before moving from East Tupelo to Mill Town in South Tupelo. They moved in with relatives, Frank and Leona Richards, on Maple Street. This helped Gladys because she was in easy walking distance of the Tupelo Garment Company where she was employed. Gladys had relatives living in South Tupelo, and Vernon had relatives living in East Tupelo. After Vernon was released from prison in February of 1939, he and Gladys seemed to have stayed in the Mill Town area of South Tupelo until Vernon's father, Jesse Dee Presley, left East Tupelo in 1942 or 1943. Jesse Dee Presley had refused to bail Vernon out of jail in November of 1937, and we do not believe the father and son ever reconciled.

During and after WWII, housing and cars were in short supply around Tupelo. In 1945, my family moved from South Tupelo into a big white wooden farmhouse on Chesterville Road west of the Tupelo airport. We lived there with my grandparents, Noon and Winnie Davis Riley for three years. Living on this small farm west of the Tupelo airport, was a great experience for my younger brother Larry and myself. Close family was around all the time, and I was one spoiled little boy. We believe this to be a similar situation as Elvis would have experienced as a child. Gladys had relatives in South Tupelo and there was little Elvis getting all the attention from his mother and relatives that a child could want. He was to seek this same constant attention for the rest of his life.

The Roots of Elvis

Every Sunday all of my aunts, uncles, and cousins would come to Grandpa Riley's house for Sunday dinner. We always had cornbread, fried chicken, and banana pudding. Every Sunday was like a family reunion. This was a common practice in the south, and provided a time to get to know your relatives. When you were introduced to someone's parents, they would always want to know who were your parents and other relatives. Neither Gladys nor Vernon seems to have known anything about the history of their families other than the Lee and Itawamba County connections. The Riley family gatherings on Sundays continued until 1965 when my grandfather died. Before 1948, my Uncle Leon Riley and Aunt Jo Ann Riley were still living at home with my grandparents. They both spent a lot of time playing with my brother, Larry, and me. We have not found Jesse Dee Presley and Vernon to have this type of close relationship with the other members of the Presley family. We have found hundreds of pictures of the Presley family gatherings in Lee and Itawamba Counties, but we have not found one picture of Jesse Dee, Vernon, or Gladys at any of these family gatherings. Minnie Mae Hood Presley does show up in some of the pictures, so we know the family was aware of the family gatherings. For some reason Jesse Dee Presley's family did not associate with the other members of the Presley family.

My uncle Leon Riley worked for Tupelo Hardware in Tupelo for over 50 years. Tupelo Hardware can trace its roots back to the Raymond and Trice Company that started in Richmond, Mississippi. Uncle Leon knew where every item in the store was located, and if Tupelo Hardware did not have the item, he could tell you where to find it.

The Roots of Elvis

Tupelo Hardware As It Looked When Elvis Received

The Guitar For His Birthday

Leon Riley was a good gentle man who spent his life helping others. For many Elvis Presley fans, Leon Riley was the man who told them the story of Gladys Presley buying her young son a guitar for his birthday. We believe that Elvis received the guitar for his eleventh birthday in January of 1946. Elvis had performed in a talent contest at the Mississippi Alabama Fair and Dairy Show in the fall of 1945. Elvis won fifth place in the contest and the girl, Mittie Pearl Payne, who won second place, had a guitar; Elvis did not. For his next birthday, Elvis got his guitar. Forrest Bobo was the Tupelo Hardware clerk who sold the guitar to Gladys Presley. Forrest Bobo's sister, Audrey Bobo, was married to William David

Pendergast. William's mother was Duskey Presley, a niece of Rosella Presley and a relative of Elvis Presley. As a child, any trip we made to Tupelo meant a visit to Tupelo Hardware where I remember standing at the large display case full of pocketknives and dreaming of having one.

Mittie Pearl 'Nubin' Payne Won Second Place. Courtesy Of Teresa Adams daughter of Shirley Mae Ellis, first cousin of Nubin Payne.

In the summer of 1948, my family moved from my grandparent's home to our own home in Verona, Mississippi. The Presley family moved this same year from Tupelo, Mississippi to Memphis, Tennessee. My Uncle Tyson and Aunt Evie Hodges had owned a small country grocery store in Verona for several years. This store was in a large house, where the family could live in the back of the house and operate the store in the front part of the house. Many small grocery stores were operated this way before the 1960's. As business grew, more of the building became store and less of a house. My first cousin, Joe Hodges, grew up in this house. Joe was 18 days older than me, and we grew up together, more like brothers than cousins, much the same as Elvis and his cousin Gene Smith. Until we were 21, most everything we did we did together. Joe was my hero, and later became a military hero in the Viet Nam war. He was awarded the Silver Star and many other service metals. Joe was a huge Elvis fan, and attended many of his concerts.

Joe Hodges, Mike West, And Julian Riley In June 2008 At The Reenactment Of Vernon and Gladys Marriage We Started In The First Grade Together At Verona And Finished High School Together At Tupelo High School

Joe Hodges died December15, 2009, on my birthday.

Hodges grocery store in Verona is where many of the local kids would hang out in the 1950s. All the business was done on credit, and you could call in your order and Evie or Tyson would deliver the groceries at no charge. Evie was the keeper of all the local gossip for Verona, so we always knew all the inside information. Joe Hodges, Mike West, and I started in the first grade together, in 1948, and continued through high school and college together. Our little gang also included my brother Larry Riley and later we included Jimmy Williams, a friend from Plantersville. Jimmy's great, grandfather was the Justice of the Peace who married Gladys and Vernon Presley. Just about everything we did or every place we went started at Hodges Grocery Store. Next door, across Main Street, was the Williams Sinclair service station. This was a typical small town service station where you always had a group of local men hanging around talking politics, basketball scores, and local gossip. The Sam Young family owned a store across the street on the northeast corner of Main Street and Raymond Street. Boyce Crouch operated a store just north of Hodges Grocery. A local bus line made the trip from Verona to Tupelo several times each day. Trips to Tupelo started by catching the bus at Hodges Grocery, and paying the dime for the ride. When we were allowed to ride without our parent's supervision, we felt we had grown up. Every Saturday was a trip to Tupelo to see a movie at the Lyric or the Tupelo theaters. These are the same two movie theaters where Elvis and his friends viewed their favorite movie stars. We could see a double feature for a dime, and then always a visit with Uncle Leon at Tupelo Hardware.

My father worked for the Tupelo Daily Journal

newspaper and my mother was the manager of the Verona school cafeteria. My friends and I lived the same small Mississippi town experience in Verona that Elvis had lived in South Tupelo and in East Tupelo. Verona was chartered in 1860, and is the oldest town in Lee County. Verona had many old buildings for us to explore, and plenty of places we could ride our horses in search of adventure. My grandfather, Noon Riley, always made sure that my cousin, Joe Hodges, my brother Larry and I had good horses when we were teenagers. In the early1930's, Noon Riley owned one of the first used car business's in Tupelo. It was located at 136 East Main Street in front of today's Tupelo City Hall. This was near where Vernon's family would live in the late 1940's. Later Grandpa Riley would own a livestock trade barn at 334 North Commerce Street in the Shake Rag area of Tupelo. Shake Rag was an area of Tupelo north of East Main Street and east of the G M & O railroad. This was an area of Tupelo where the poorest of the black families lived. The area had dirt roads, no indoor plumbing, and very poor housing. A shack is the best way to describe the housing available in this part of Tupelo. My Grandpa Riley's livestock barn was located in Shake Rag where the Bancorp South Arena is now sitting. After leaving East Tupelo, about 1947, Vernon's family lived for a short time on the corner of Commerce and East Main Street in a house facing Main Street. This was on the edge of Shake Rag, but was not in the Shake Rag area, as some would have you believe. At that time, Vernon was working for L. P. McCarty wholesale grocery and was living across the street from the business. Vernon's family next moved to Mulberry Alley, south of Main Street behind the L. P. McCarty and the Cockrell Banana Company. Mulberry Alley ran east and west and stopped on the west end at the G M & O railroad. This site is now in front of the Tupelo City Hall building. Both the Commerce Street and the Mulberry Alley locations were within two blocks of downtown Tupelo, and were in easy walking distance of Gladys and Vernon's employment.

On Sundays, Grandpa Riley would take the young grandchildren with him to feed and water the animals at his livestock barn in Tupelo. When he had a good horse, he would saddle it and let us ride around the streets of Shake Rag. I do not remember ever hearing any music the times I was in the area. Shake Rag was not an area that Gladys would have allowed Elvis to visit without her supervision and they never lived there. It would be a mistake to consider all the black areas of Tupelo as Shake Rag.

The first time I ever heard of Elvis Presley, my father had come home from work at the Tupelo newspaper and was in the kitchen with my mother. He was telling her about a boy from East Tupelo who had a big hit record, and was getting to be very popular in the Memphis area. I do not know why this conversation stuck in my head.

Gladys Smith Presley had been friends with my Aunt Zora Mears Riley for a long time. Gladys and Zora had lived near each other, east of Saltillo, when they were young girls. They had attended some school together, and both of their families had to struggle to survive. Zora's parents, Norman and Daisy Mears, had moved to East Tupelo in the early 1930s. They lived on East Main Street where Palmers Big Star is located today. After Gladys father, Bob Smith, died about 1931 or

1932, the Smith family moved to the northeast corner lot on Berry and Adams Street in East Tupelo. Gladys, like many of the local farm girls, was working for the Tupelo Garment Company. To find employees, the Tupelo Garment Company had in the beginning sent buses out into the county to pick up and transport farm girls into Tupelo to work at the Garment Company. This was a great source of year round employment for young women in the 1930's. Gladys was one of the girls riding the bus into Tupelo to work as a sewing machine operator at the Tupelo Garment Company. It was here that she met Faye Harris, who was to become her close friend for life. When Gladys arrived in East Tupelo, she already had girl friends to show her around town. Faye Harris and Zora Riley were two of the local girls that would travel with Gladys and Elvis on Noah Presley's school bus to Parchman to visit Vernon in prison. After the Presley family moved to Memphis, Gladys and Elvis would often return to East Tupelo to visit with her family and friends. Some of the memories people have of Elvis in East Tupelo were after the family had moved to Memphis. After Elvis became very popular, Gladys and Elvis could not come back to East Tupelo to visit. Gladys had a very hard life in Tupelo before moving to Memphis, but she always wanted to return home to her friends and family in East Tupelo.

In August of 1997, Zora Riley was interviewed by Michaela Morris, with the Northeast Mississippi Daily Journal. Zora said, "My mother, Daisy Mears, was called on to help when Gladys Presley went into labor with Elvis and his twin brother. My mother pinned the first diaper on Elvis. Elvis' music talent began showing up when he was just a small child. He would drag out buckets and lids, turning them into a drum set. He was always singing and jumping around. He always wanted to be in school plays. During the bus rides to visit his father, who was serving a prison sentence, young Elvis would raid the box lunches packed by the girls for the trip. Half the time he would eat the dinner before we got there. After the Presley family moved to Memphis, they would come back to East Tupelo and visit with us. We would have hamburger suppers, they were good times. I remember Elvis would go rabbit hunting with my sons. Elvis was a good child and he told me that he would always be an East Tupelo boy." Zora Riley lived in East Tupelo until she died in 2002 with many of her stories of East Tupelo and Elvis stories untold. We believe what Elvis said was true; he was always an East Tupelo boy.

Rockwell Youth Center In Tupelo

In 1954, Rockwell Manufacturing Company provided the money to build a youth center at City Park on Joyner Street in Tupelo. In the 1950's and 60's, the Youth Center provided the teenagers around Tupelo, a wonderful gathering place. Before we could drive, Aunt Evie Hodges would pile all the local Verona kids into the old Plymouth station wagon and take us to the youth center. We had dances after the football games, parties every weekend, and a great place to take our date after a movie. We experienced the birth of rock and roll from the dance floor of the Rockwell Youth Center. I can still hear the jukebox playing "Don't Be Cruel", "Hound Dog", and "Johnny Be Good". The 1950s had to be the best time ever to be a teenager.

A Friday Night Party At Rockwell Youth Center In 1959

I was lucky to have seen Elvis perform live two times at the Mississippi Alabama Fair and Dairy Show. If I had to pick two times to see him, I guess the 1956 and 1957 performances would have been the best choices. The first time Elvis performed the song "Jailhouse Rock" live was at the 1957 Fair and Dairy Show. As you walked around the fairgrounds in 1957, every booth had a

45-record player and everyone was playing the song, "Jailhouse Rock". Aunt Evie Hodges had made me a red velvet shirt just like the one Elvis had worn at the concert in 1956. I sure wish that I could remember what happened to that shirt.

    As a young man, I developed an interest in the early history of Verona and its founding families. Verona is the oldest chartered town in Lee County, and is the birthplace of many of the oldest businesses in Tupelo. The small town of Verona has produced three United States Congressmen, and many more prominent business leaders. In 1991, I purchased two of the three oldest buildings in Verona. Having been constructed about 1860, these were also the oldest buildings left in Lee County. One of the buildings had served as the City of Verona Post Office until 1951; the other building is the original location of Raymond and Trice General Merchandise. This business would later move to Tupelo as Trice Raymond Hardware. This hardware business would be sold to the Booth family and would become famous as Tupelo Hardware, where Elvis Presley purchased his first guitar. This old Verona building was also the location of the first bank in Lee County. Raymond and Trice Banking House had its origins in Richmond, Mississippi and was chartered as a bank in Verona, Mississippi in 1876. The bank was moved to Tupelo, Mississippi in 1886 as the Bank of Tupelo, and is still operated in Tupelo as Bancorp South. Over the years, the old building in Verona had served the community for many purposes. The third one of the old buildings had been used as the Verona Town Hall from 1860 until 1976. For 25 years, the building was used as a church downstairs and continued to serve as the Masonic Lodge upstairs. When the building was offered for sale in 2004, I purchased the building because I owned the other two adjoining buildings, and did not want to see any of the buildings torn down. In addition, my research had revealed that Gladys Smith and Vernon Presley were married in Verona, Mississippi on June 17, 1933, by Justice of the Peace, Robert Emmit Kelly. In a 1956 interview, Vernon and Gladys stated that they had run off to Verona to get married. Faye Harris, one of Gladys good friends from East Tupelo, stated in an interview that Gladys and Vernon ran off to Verona to get married. Because of this historic event, I started a restoration project in 2004 of all three old buildings. This restoration project has been an experience and a story by itself. Our goal was to have a place Elvis fans can visit which has a feel of the time when Gladys and Vernon Presley were married there. We now have a restaurant and an antique shop in two of the buildings and a museum in the third one. Mrs. Ruth's Dinner in Verona has become a stopping place for many Elvis Presley fans. They can get a southern cooked meal just as Elvis would have eaten; look at all of the Elvis memorabilia, have their picture taken and write their names on the restaurant wall.

In December 2005, the local TV station ran a story about the old Verona Town Hall Building and the Elvis Presley family connection. On December 22, 2005, Rachel Ann Harden came walking in the front door of the Old Town Hall. Rachel Ann has been interested in everything Elvis for most of her life, but she did not know Gladys and Vernon had been married in Verona, Mississippi. Rachel Ann had lived in Verona after she graduated from the University of Mississippi. I was impressed with her knowledge of Elvis Presley history. Rachel Ann's

The Roots of Elvis

earliest memory of Elvis was the 1973 TV special "Aloha from Hawaii". This show was all that was required to make her a full time Elvis fan. She collects Elvis books and nothing thrills her more that to find an Elvis picture or some other original Elvis artifact. The more she learned about Elvis, the more interested she became in his family. Rachel Ann had become good friends with Brother Frank Smith, pastor of the First Assembly of God Church in East Tupelo in 1945. This was a church in East Tupelo attended by the Presley family. Reverend Smith helped Elvis learn to play the guitar, and this church was the first place Elvis ever sang in public. This small church was located on the southeast corner of Berry and Adams Street in East Tupelo. This old small wooden church still survives and had been used as a residence on Berry Street since 1958. The church was moved in 1958 to create room for a church that sits at that location today. In 2008, the Birth Place Museum purchased the old church, moved it from Berry Street, and restored it to its former look. Visitors to the Birthplace Museum can now experience the look and feel of attending a small country church in East Tupelo in the 1940's.

Because of my efforts to restore the old buildings in Verona, I was invited to speak to the Itawamba Historical society on February 12, 2006. Before 1867, Verona and Tupelo were both a part of Itawamba County. The subject of the program was to be the building restoration project in Verona. As my talks usually go, I touched on several subjects. One was the story of Gladys Smith and Vernon Presley running off to Verona, Mississippi on June 17, 1933 to get married. The young couple first went to Pontotoc County to apply for the marriage license

The Roots of Elvis

because Vernon was only 17 years old. This could have caused them a problem in Lee County or Itawamba County. After lying about their ages, and getting the marriage license they were driven back to Verona by Marshall and Vona Mae Presley Brown, and were married by Justice of the Peace Robert Emmit Kelly who lived in Verona, Mississippi. Mr. Kelly had married Marshall and Vona Mae in Verona, so they knew the procedure. Vona Mae was a first cousin to Vernon, and Marshall was a distant cousin to Gladys Smith.

After the Historical Society meeting was over, Charles and Virble Booth from Itawamba County, told me a story about Elvis Presley's great grandfather living in Itawamba County, Mississippi. At the time, I was not aware that the Presley family was from Itawamba County. I did not know that Elvis Presley's great grandmother, Rosella, never married, but was mother to nine children. I had been a fan of Elvis since 1955, but all I had ever heard was Tupelo, birthplace of Elvis Presley. Charles Booth gave me the name and telephone number of a man who was supposed to be related to the great grandfather of Elvis Presley. Elvis's great grandfather lived in and was buried in the north part of Itawamba County. I did not know what to think about this story, or what to believe. How could this information have not been previously recorded and reported? I thanked the couple, wrote down the information, put it into my pocket, and made my way to the refreshment table. When I returned home, I put the information in my dresser drawer and did not think about it for several months.

On March 23, 2006, Rachel Ann and Buddy Palmer

The Roots of Elvis

organized a meeting, at the Old Town Hall in Verona, of local people with Elvis stories to tell. We recorded as many of the stories as we could get. Buddy Palmer is a long time friend of mine who lives and owned a business in East Tupelo. Buddy personally knew many members of the Presley family. One of the people who showed up to tell his stories was Hal of Fame rockabilly star Gene Simmons. Gene had gone to school at Verona High School, and had many interesting stories about the early days of rock and roll. I can remember Gene sitting in the stands of the Verona School gym with his guitar and girls all around. Gene and his brothers had a band that would play at the old Verona school gym. This was 1952 to 1953 and rhythm and blues music was becoming popular with the young fans. At that time, we had no idea what was about to happen to the music world.

Gene played as an opening act for Elvis in the early 1950's, and would later play with the Bill Black Combo, Elvis set up a recording session for Gene at the Sun Studio in Memphis in 1958. Sun released one of Gene's songs, but it was not a hit. Gene moved to Hi Records and had a hit song with "Haunted House" in 1964. The song went to number 11 on the Hot 100. In 1994, Gene Simmons and Tommy Barnes wrote a song called "Indian Outlaw". This song was to become Tim McGraw's first big hit. Gene Simmons was selected as a member of the Rockabilly Hall Of Fame.

One of the stories Gene told us was of the June 15, 1955 concert at the Belden School gym. The stage was set up at the back of the gym and there was no back door for Elvis to enter.

The Roots of Elvis

Elvis wanted to make his entrance from the back of the stage. Some of the fans opened a window to the boys bathroom so that Elvis could crawl through. Gene said Elvis was wearing pink pants that night. As Elvis crawled through the window, he tore the seat of his pants. Girls in the 50's always carried safety pins with them just in case they needed to make on the spot repairs. Gene and some others went through the stands collecting safety pins to repair the seat of Elvis's pants. At this time, Elvis had been performing for less than one year.

This meeting at the Old Town Hall was the last public appearance of Gene Simmons. Two weeks later Gene was diagnosed with cancer. Gene Simmons died in Tupelo, Mississippi, August 29, 2006. We miss him.

**Gene Simmons And His Band In The Early 1950's
Courtesy Of Dorothy Lyons**

The Roots of Elvis

Whit Presley with Elvis After The 1956 Show At The Mid South Fair In Tupelo.   Whit Was One Of The Guards Courtesy Of Margaret Little

Gene Simmons, Billy Boren And Other Verona Students In The Gym   About 1953   Courtesy Of   Billy Boren

Pocket Full Of Rainbows

After listening to Rachel Ann talk about Elvis and his family, I started to put that information into a family tree. Genealogy is another passion of mine and this family tree was going to be a challenge. During the spring of 2006, Rachel Ann and I started to work on a complete family tree for Elvis Presley. We could not believe that no one had done this complete Presley research before. Many people had worked on various parts of this tree, but no one had put it all together. Roy Turner is the only local person that had researched the family tree. Most of Roy's research was into the Smith and Mansell families, and was conducted before the 1920 and 1930 census records were available. After getting several hundred names in the family tree, I remembered the name and phone number I had placed in the dresser drawer, so we decided to give Mackey Hargett a phone call. In May 2006, we called the number and spoke with Peggy Hargett, wife of Mackey Hargett. She explained that the man believed to be the father of Jessie Dee McDowell Presley was a John Wallace from Itawamba County. John Wallace was born August 1, 1853 in the Union Grove - Tilden community of Itawamba County, Mississippi. This is about seven miles south of Fulton, Mississippi. Peggy invited us to come over to her home in the Fairview Community in the north part of Itawamba County. We did not meet Mackey this trip because he was building a house, but we did meet Peggy at the Salem Church cemetery in Itawamba County. She showed us the grave of John Wallace and gave us a picture of him as a young man. John Wallace died November 17, 1935 and is buried at Salem Cemetery in Itawamba County. The GPS location is 34 degrees 25.033 minutes North and 88 degrees 17.660 minutes west. John Wallace was a good-looking young man and he was a musician. John was one of the local fiddle players. In the days of no television or radio for entertainment, southern people gathered at barn dances, picnics, and church events to socialize. A handsome musician such as John Wallace would have been popular with the young women. We thanked Peggy for her time and information, and arranged to meet with her husband a few weeks later.

On June 11, 2006, we met Mackey and Peggy Hargett at their home in the Fairview Community of Itawamba County. Mackey explained that his grandmother, Elnora Wallace Yarber, was the oldest daughter of John Wallace. After Elvis Presley became popular, Mackey's grandmother as well as her brother and sisters, told the family that they were related to Elvis Presley. They explained that they had a half brother named Jesse Dee McDowell Presley, Elvis's grandfather. Rosella Presley, Elvis's great grandmother, never married but she was mother to nine children. All her children took the Presley name, but all had fathers with other names. Had Elvis not become famous, this family secret would probably have died with that generation. All the Wallace family called their half brother 'Dee'. Mrs. Elnora said that John Wallace acknowledged Jesse Dee as his son and would give him money when Jesse would come to his house. It is understandable that Rosella would send Jesse Dee to his father's house for money. As a single mother, sharecropping with a house full of children, Rosella never had enough money. We believe that Rosella's children knew who their fathers were. They lived in a small community, and in a small house; they had to know who was coming to visit their mother. Proof of that is when Jesse Dee Presley remarried in Kentucky on December 4, 1948, the marriage application records that Jesse Dee's father was John Presley. There never was a John Presley in Itawamba County, but there was a John Wallace. Jesse Dee's mother was a Presley, not his father. Jesse Dee did not want his new wife to know he was illegitimate, so he lied about his father's last name. This has caused confusion for many people researching the Elvis Presley family tree. Many have tried to find a John Presley married to Rosella Presley. Some have even made up a marriage to John Presley, but that never happened. Jesse Dee's mother was named Presley, not his father. We were later told this same story about John Wallace by relatives of John's third daughter, Robbie Wallace. These relatives live in Arkansas, but they related the same story as the ones living in Itawamba County.

**John Wallace
Elvis Presley And Mackey Hargett's Great Grandfather In
His Early 20's. Courtesy Mackey Hargett**

For The Good Times

Mackey was happy for a chance to tell us his story, and he gave us permission to use the story if we were to write a book. In 1956, Elvis was becoming famous around the world. Mackey's grandmother, Elnora Wallace, and his mother, Lillian Yarber Hargett, told him a story about Elvis Presley being his cousin and the history behind the family relationship. Lillian Yarber was born October 24, 1905 in Itawamba County, Mississippi and died January 23, 1989 in Tishomingo County, Mississippi. Mackey was born on August 24, 1943 in Tupelo, Mississippi at the Tupelo Hospital. When Mackey's father, Tearsie Hargett, joined the army in World War II, Mackey and his mother moved back to Belmont, Mississippi and lived with Mackey's grandparents. Tearsie Hargett was born on August 12, 1910 in Marion County, Alabama and was killed July 18, 1944 while serving his country fighting with the 3rd Armored Tank Division under General George Patton in France. At the time of Mackey's birth, his mother Lillian was living in East Tupelo, in the same area on the old Saltillo Road that Vernon and Gladys Presley had lived. Tearsie Hargett worked as a projectionist at the Lyric Theater on Broadway Street in Tupelo across the street from the courthouse. The Lyric Theater is one of the two movie theaters that Elvis would attend when he was a child. The other was the Tupelo Theater located on the south side of Main Street, across the street from Tupelo Hardware. This was originally known as the Strand. On Saturday, Elvis could see two movies for a dime. His dream of becoming an entertainer would have started while watching movies at these two theaters.

The Roots of Elvis

**Lillian Hargett, Mackey's Hargett's Mother.
Photo Made In Tupelo When She Was In Her Early 20's.**

Lillian And Tearsie Hargett

Lillian Hargett And Vester Presley On The Driveway Close To Gates Of Graceland. Photo Taken By Mackey Hargett.

Lillian Hargett And Patsy Presley

The Roots of Elvis

East Tupelo is where Lillian and Tearsie lived when they met and were married. Mackey did not know his father and he grew up as an only child, much the same as Elvis. Mackey attended school in Belmont, Mississippi until 1953. That year Lillian met Garland B. Nevels when he was working in Itawamba County constructing highway 25 from Fulton to Belmont. Lillian and Garland married that same year and moved to Brookhaven, Mississippi. Mackey attended high school in Brookhaven. Lillian and Mackey would continue to visit his grandparents in Belmont. In 1956, Elvis was becoming famous, and Mackey's grandmother told him a family secret that no one had talked about. Finding out that he had some unknown close relatives was very important to Mackey. The fact that he had a relative who was becoming famous was very exciting to this young Mississippi boy. As a teenager, Mackey wished he could visit Graceland and visit his famous relatives. In mid 1960, after he got his driver's license, Mackey and his mother made the trip to Memphis to visit Graceland. Mrs. Lillian explained to the gatekeeper who she was, and they were allowed to drive right to the front door of Graceland. Vernon and Vester remembered Lillian Hargett living in the same area of East Tupelo where they had lived. Elvis was not at home when they made this first visit, but Vernon invited them to come back another time so he could introduce them to Elvis. Vernon showed them around, and gave them his telephone number so Mackey could call before they made another trip to Graceland. On a latter trip, Lillian had her picture taken with Vester and Mackey had his picture taken with Anita Wood and Vernon's sister Nash. They all thought that Lillian and Nash looked like sisters. At this time, Anita Wood was Elvis's girlfriend.

The Roots of Elvis

In the spring of 1963, Mackey made another trip to Graceland and this time he was introduced to Elvis. Mackey was sitting in the living room at Graceland when Vernon asked him to come back to the kitchen. Elvis came down the back staircase into the kitchen and Vernon introduced them saying, "Elvis, this is a cousin of yours on the Wallace side of the family." This introduction was very exciting and important for a young man from the hills of Itawamba County to hear while in the presence of his cousin, Elvis Presley. Mackey was in the kitchen with Vernon and Elvis when Vernon gave Elvis a small pearl handle pistol. Elvis stuck the pistol in his belt. Mackey was allowed to hang out at Graceland with all the friends and family members. Later that night they all went to the Memphis fairgrounds. Elvis would rent the fairgrounds after closing time for all his friends to gather and have fun. Mackey has a picture of Elvis at the fairground with the pearl handle pistol stuck in his belt. This night Elvis had a date with a young dark haired girl that Mackey did not know. Mackey remembers her coming down from upstairs at Graceland, as they were getting ready to leave for the fairgrounds. This girl turned out to be Priscilla Beaulieu who would later marry Elvis. Cousins Billy Smith and Gene Smith were also at the fairgrounds that night. Mackey was allowed to take pictures of anything, or anyone that he wanted to. This was special because the family did not allow many people to take pictures inside Graceland.

The Roots of Elvis

Elvis Presley, Red West, a very young Priscilla in the background and cousin Billy Smith, photo taken at the Memphis Fairgrounds which Elvis had rented for the evening. Photo taken by Mackey Hargett.

The Roots of Elvis

Mackey Hargett And Anita Wood With Vernon's Sister Nash Standing In Front Of Mackey's Red Chevy.

Old Verona Town Hall Where Gladys Smith And Vernon Presley Were Married   June 17, 1933

The Roots of Elvis

Poolside at Graceland. Red West's wife, Minnie Mae, Nash, Dee Stanley. In back, Earl Pritchard and two daughters.

Photo taken by Mackey Hargett.

Vester Presley, Delta, Minnie Mae & Mackey Hargett. Photo Taken In Front Of 1961 Limo By Earl Prichett.

Mackey Hargett's 1960 Chevy At Graceland

Vernon's 1930 Model A Ford, 1956 Lincoln And Elvis' Pink & White Caddy Behind Graceland. Photo Taken By Mackey Hargett.

After his first visit, Mackey would visit Vernon at Graceland and other locations many times over the next eighteen years. Mackey would call Vernon, and Vernon would tell him when he could visit. Vernon never once told him no, but sometimes the visit would have to be changed to different times and dates. Vernon did not allow Mackey to bring other visitors on any of these trips. On some of the trips, Mackey would visit with Vester and his family. Sometimes Mackey would stay at Vester's house. Mackey remembers going with Vester to collect eggs at the chicken house behind Graceland. Mackey recalls Vester's address at that time as 1111 Car Avenue.

The Roots of Elvis

    Mackey was very impressed with all the cars Elvis had at Graceland, and took pictures of many of them. Before Elvis died, Vernon had a car lot and sold many of the cars that belonged to Elvis. Sometimes Mackey was invited to go to the late night movies, and the skating rink with Elvis and his friends. One of the movies he remembers was "Village of the Dammed". Another was Mickey Rooney in "It's a Mad, Mad, Mad, Mad World". Mackey said that Elvis would sing when at the Fairgrounds and that he liked to play with the bumper cars.

    One event that Mackey remembers was tragic. One Saturday night in 1961, Mackey was at Graceland hanging out with Billy and Bobby Smith. These were two of Elvis's first cousins. Mackey took Billy to visit his girl friend at her house. When he returned to Graceland, Mackey and Bobby Smith walked across Highway 51 to get some snacks. On returning, Mackey crossed the highway first and after crossing, he heard car tires screeching. When he turned around, he could see that Bobby had been hit and thrown upon the hood of a car. His legs were severely injured. Mackey remembers going to a Memphis hospital and other family members arriving. They wanted to know why Billy was not at the hospital with Bobby. Mackey remembers going back to the girlfriend's house to get Billy Smith. Bobby did survive the accident, but his injuries were a problem for him the rest of his life. Mackey remembers that the story appeared in the Sunday morning Memphis newspaper.

    After Gladys died on August 14, 1958, Vernon went with Elvis to Germany. Vernon met Dee Stanley in November of 1958 while he was in Germany. Vernon and Dee married on

July 3, 1960 in Huntsville, Alabama. Elvis did not attend the wedding. Vernon moved Dee and her three boys into Graceland, where they lived until December of 1961. Mackey first met Dee and her three boys, Billy, Ricky, and David Stanley when they lived with Vernon at Graceland. He has pictures of the boys in the swimming pool with Vernon. He also has pictures of the boy's bicycles beside Elvis's motorcycle. Vernon, Dee and her boys lived at Graceland for less than two years.

Mackey Hargett Family   About 1972

The Roots of Elvis

Mackey was married to Sherry Moore on February 4, 1966, and they had three children. Anna Maria Hargett was born November 17, 1969, Matthew Edward Hargett was born December 8, 1966, and Joel Rue Hargett was born February 3, 1971. Sherry went to Graceland with Mackey to visit about three times. In mid 1974, Mackey took his daughter, Anna Maria, to Memphis where she had her picture taken with Vernon and with Dee. Mackey and Sherry were divorced in 1975. Over the years, Mackey visited Vernon and Dee at their homes on Hermitage and 1266 Dolan Drive. The house on Dolan Drive backs up to Graceland with a gate in the back yard that gave access to the grounds of Graceland. After Mackey was married, his trips to visit Graceland slowed down to about twice a year. Most of the time Elvis was not at home, so Mackey stayed with Vernon or Vester. Sometimes Mackey would just drive to Memphis and back the same day. On one of the last visits, in June of 1974, Mackey went to Vernon's house to find Vernon had moved out and was living with Sandy Miller at 1293 Old Hickory Road. After Vernon and Dee's separation, Vernon purchased Dee's interest in their house on Dolan Drive. By the end of 1976, Vernon was showing signs of being a sick man. Mackey visited Vernon for the last time in 1978, not long before Vernon died. At that time, Vernon and Sandy were living at the house on 1293 Old Hickory Road. The last picture of Mackey and Vernon together was taken by Sandy Miller at this house.

Mackey never went to an Elvis concert, but he has memories of visiting with Minnie Mae, Vernon, Elvis, Vester, Patsy (Vester's daughter), Delta, Nash, and the Smith boys. He will always be grateful for their kindness in taking the time to visit with him at Graceland. They always treated him as a member of the family, and those memories will stay with him forever.

Sitting in Mackey and Peggy's kitchen, listening to him tell all his stories was almost unbelievable, but the best was yet to come. Peggy left the room and came back with a box of pictures that we had never expected to see. To our amazement, they produced dozens of pictures of Mackey's visits with Vernon. Elvis, Anita Wood, Red West, Vernon, Vester, Minnie Mae, Dee, Priscilla, the Smith cousins, and others were in the photos. Most of these pictures are unpublished. Mackey has graciously allowed us to use the pictures on our web site and in this book. We are very lucky to have found Mackey. Without his information, a very important part of the Elvis Presley story might have been lost.

Mackey Hargett With Pink Jeep From Blue Hawaii, Three Bicycles, Pink Caddy, Lincoln And Model A Ford.

Mackey Hargett With Elvis's Cadillac Limo

Elvis's Girlfriend Anita Wood Was Also A Friend Of Billy Boren, Brother Of Charlie Boren, Elvis's Friend At WELO

The Roots of Elvis

Back of Graceland, see Vernon's '56 Lincoln, '56 Pink & White Caddy, 3 bicycles and Elvis' motorcycle. Photo taken by Mackey Hargett.

51

The Roots of Elvis

Photo Taken By Red West Of Mackey, Elvis & Lamar Fike Inside The Car On Their Way To See 'Wild in the Country'

**Vester Presley And Mackey Hargett
Photo Taken By Lillian Hargett.**

In The background – What The Other Side Of Hwy 51 Looked Like In The 1960's.

Mackey Hargett

Mackey Hargett In Front Of Graceland

**Patsy Presley And Mackey Hargett In Front Of Graceland About 1972.
Photo Taken By Sherrie Moore Hargett.**

Dee Stanley Presley With Maria Hargett In 1974. Photo At Dolan Street Taken By Mackey Hargett.

At Graceland Mackey With Elvis Motorcycle. Photo Taken Sunday Morning by Vester Presley.

The Roots of Elvis

Vernon Presley Holding Maria Hargett In 1974 In Front Of Sandy Miller's House Photo Taken By Mackey Hargett.

Vernon Presley & Mackey Hargett Summer Of 1974. Photo Taken At Dolan Street By Sandy Miller. Vernon's Belt Buckle Has EP On It.

VISITS PRESLEY—Recently Vernon Presley, father of the late Elvis Presley, invited Mackey to visit with him at the Presley home.

Last Picture Taken Of Vernon Presley And Mackey Hargett Photo Taken By Sandy Miller At Dolan Street In 1978.

Mackey Hargett And Vernon Presley At Dolan Street In The Mid 1970's.   Photo Taken By Sherry Hargett.

Blue Eyed Handsome Man

After receiving all this information from Mackey, we started our search for John Wallace and his connection to Rosella Presley. We believe that John Wallace could be the father of several of Rosella's children. John was born August 1, 1853 about six miles south of Fulton in the Union Grove community of Itawamba County, Mississippi. John's parents were Hugh Wallace and Lydia Gideon Wallace. Many members of the Wallace family lived in the southern part of Itawamba County. Hugh Wallace and Lydia Gideon were married in Itawamba County on October 6, 1852. John had a younger brother Willis Wallace, born in 1859, and two younger sisters. Malinda Wallace was born in 1856 and Mollie Wallace was born in 1858. John's mother, Lydia Gideon Wallace, died about 1859 in Itawamba County. We have not found Lydia's burial site, but it should be somewhere in the Tilden community. John's father Hugh Wallace married Mary Forrester on January 3, 1861. John would have been about 8 years old at that time. John worked on the family farm and lived in the Tilden community until he was about 22 years old. We do not believe John could read or write, because on several documents he made an X for his signature. Sometime after 1870, John Wallace moved from Itawamba County to Collin Texas. After the War for Southern Independence, the South was living under forced reconstruction and many young men left Mississippi and migrated to Texas. John lived in Texas for about three years when he met and then married Rachel Barlough on August 9, 1877. The marriage was performed by John McKinney and is recorded in book 4, page 181. Rachel was born in 1859 at Hickory Hill, Titus County,

Texas. Her father was John Hamilton Barlough and her mother was Delilah C. Bennett. John Barlough was born in 1810 in South Carolina. Delilah was born in 1823 in Georgia. John Barlough had served in the U S Army and received a land grant in Texas in 1854. Rachel had two older sisters, Sarah A. was born in 1854, and Louisa was born in 1858. Delilah Bennett Barlough died in 1874, and John Barlough married Paralee Simmons March 18, 1875. Paralee Simmons was not much older than John Barlough's daughters were. After the War for Southern Independence, it was common for older men to marry much younger women because many young men had been killed in the War.

John Wallace and Rachel Barlough had one son born in Texas. George Hugh Wallace was born about 1878. On the June 1880 census, John Wallace is living in Collin, Texas and is a widower. We believe John's first wife Rachel may have died from complications of childbirth. We have not found George Hugh Wallace on any record after the 1880 census, and family members report that he died at a young age. After the death of Rachel, John is left with a small child to take care of. For several reasons John and his son leave Texas after June 1880 and move back to Tilden in Itawamba County, Mississippi. We believe that John's relatives back in Itawamba County encouraged him to come back to Mississippi. John was a young single man without a wife and he needed help with his young child. Moving back to Mississippi was a good decision. Had John Wallace not moved back to Mississippi, we would not have had an Elvis Presley.

The Roots of Elvis

On December 23, 1880, John Wallace married Elmira Jane McFadden. The McFadden families were early settlers of the Tilden community, and owned hundreds of acres of land in the area. Elmira's father had been killed in the War for Southern Independence and she needed a husband to help her care for the farm. John was a widower with a young child. He needed a wife to help him care for his young son. This marriage was a good match for both John Wallace and Elmira McFadden.

John and Elmira Jane raised a family of nine children. Elnora Wallace was born September 1, 1882, Bettie Lovie Wallace was born in March, 1885, Robbie C Wallace was born in August 1886, Ausie Howard Wallace was born June 18, 1888, John Kirby Wallace was born October 24, 1889, Selma Ann Wallace was born in November 1891, Jessie Pearl Wallace was born April 21, 1895, Willie Mae Wallace was born February 1898, and Archie Homer Wallace was born February 12, 1903.

John Wallace was a handsome young man, and was a very good fiddle player. In rural Mississippi, the local musician would have been a very popular man. He would have been viewed as the rock stars of today. We believe that the local girls would have liked John, just as they like the rock stars of today. John would have played at the barn dances, church socials, and local parties. He also would have played at the White Springs Resort just down the road from Rosella and Rosalinda Presley.

Elmira Jane McFadden Wallace With Children Willie, Jessie And Homer

The Roots of Elvis

John Wallace and Family

John Wallace and Elmira

John Wallace Homer, Carle, Ausie, Kelly, Homer's Boy, And Mildred   Courtesy Of Mackey Hargett

The Roots of Elvis

Brothers Calhoun, Mack, And Jesse Dee Presley   Jesse Dee In Uniform   Courtesy Of Patsy Presley Pressnall

Elnora, Lovie, Jessie and Willie Wallace

Heartbreak Hotel

About two miles west of Tilden, on the banks to the Tombigbee River, was a resort known as White Springs. White Springs was named for the four mineral springs that flowed into the river from the surrounding hills. As early as 1850, people were coming to bath in and drink the healthy mineral water. The resort included 2 hotels, a dance hall, a saloon, 25 cabins for rent, a general store, many bathhouses built along the river, and a ferry. The resort covered about 80 acres. Many dances and political gatherings were held at White Springs and we believe John Wallace was a popular musician at these events. The wealthy people from all over the area would have been staying at the White Spring resort.

Our research into the two Presley sisters, Rosella and Rosalinda, has revealed that they were having affairs with wealthy men. These men could help support and care for them and their children. Two young girls and a grandmother would have had to have some help to survive in rural Mississippi. What we had a problem with, was how did the two girls meet the wealthy men? They lived two miles down a dirt road in a remote part of Itawamba County. The Wallace, McFadden, Steele, Bowen, Reed, and Presley families all lived as neighbors in the Tilden community. They would have worked together, attended church, and local social gatherings together. In 1880, John Wallace's brother, Willis Wallace, John's grandmother and his John's aunt all lived three houses from the Presley girls on the White Springs Road, west of Tilden. We believe that Willis Wallace, younger brother of John Wallace, may have been

The Roots of Elvis

interested in Rosella Presley before John moved back to Mississippi. Willis Wallace was a close neighbor to the Presley girls on White Springs Road. Relatives told us that something happened that caused the two brothers to not speak to each other for the remainder of their lives. Willis Wallace did not marry until after the Presley girls left the Tilden community.

When I was first given a newspaper article about the White Springs resort, it answered many of the questions I had about the lives of these girls. They were not living in a remote part of Itawamba County; they were living less than two miles from White Springs, the most popular resort in Lee, Monroe, and Itawamba Counties. They went to dances and parties at the resort, and may have even worked at the resort. For over 70 years, the resort drew crowds from all over Northeast Mississippi. Today not much remains of the resort that once stood along that quite stretch of the Tombigbee River. We have found two advertisements for the resort that were run in local newspapers. The first one appeared in the Fulton Southern Herald on September 15, 1860. James M. Williams ran the ad. The ad reads; the subscriber takes this method of informing the public that he is the proprietor of the above named springs and their well-known virtues need no further recommendation than can be given by the many hundreds who have tried their healing efficacy. The springs are situated on the Tombigbee River three miles South of Van Buren and eight miles north of Smithville in a pleasant and healthy locality where there are strong inducements for indulgence in field and river sports for the well, while ample preparations are made to promote the comfort and ease of the invalid; also, arrangements for bathing and a gymnasium for exercise and a number of suitable rooms for rent.

James M. Williams was born in Jefferson County, Alabama in 1830. His father was Owen Williams. The family moved to Itawamba County, Mississippi about 1838. On the 1850 census, James is listed as a farmer, but he may have been the first person to operate the White Springs resort. By 1862, James and his family are living in Tupelo, Mississippi. The building of the M and O Railroad in 1857 caused a movement of people from Itawamba County to the towns of Tupelo and Verona in Lee County. On the 1870 census, James is living in Tupelo and is working as a Tinnier.

The second advertisement about White Springs was run in the Tupelo Journal in 1877. The ad reads: New Hotel at White Springs in Itawamba County, Mississippi. Seven miles north of Smithville, and twenty miles east of Tupelo and Verona, and ten miles south of Fulton. The undersigned will open on the first day of June 1877 the above hotel for the reception of boarders and visitors. The second ball of the season will be given on Wednesday, July 4. The proprietor announces to the invalid and the pleasure seeker that he has taken charge of the above noted watering place, and has thoroughly changed and refitted a new hotel and cabins for renters. His rooms will be newly and neatly furnished, and his table supplied with everything that the adjacent land can afford, also a meat market for renters. A string band has been engaged, and the musical department will be complete throughout the season. Game of all kinds plenty in the neighborhood, and fish in the river and lakes near the springs. Of the medicinal virtues of these springs, it is deemed unnecessary to say anything, as their properties have been analyzed and published, and tested by hundreds who visited them since their discovery thirty years ago. These springs are renowned throughout North Mississippi and their healing properties are well known. The Proprietor will spare no pains to make his guests and renters comfortable, and is determined that no one shall leave dissatisfied. Renters will be furnished with neat and comfortable cabins. Board and rent will be furnished at the most reasonable terms. Give me a call if you are in pursuit of health, sport, or fun. The rules of board and lodging are; per day $2.00, per week $10.00, per month $30.00. Cabins rent for $.50 per day, and $10.00 per month. Perfect satisfaction is guaranteed. Respectfully, Elisha Newton Fears, Proprietor May 12, 1877.

Elisha Fears was born February 13, 1842 in Lawrence County, Alabama. In 1860, he was a student in Alabama. Sometime before 1867, Elisha moved from Alabama to Smithville, Monroe County, Mississippi. In 1870, he is listed as a farmer, living in Smithville. On the 1880 census, he is listed as a clerk in a store and is living in Smithville. The management of a resort in Itawamba County must have been a hard business.

Although the springs were the main attraction, people came from all around just for the entertainment. Candidate speaking, picnics, dances, singings, hunting, and fishing, were available to visitors. Every Fourth of July there would be a picnic and celebration. Some people would go for the day and others would rent a cabin and stay for a week or more. It was a great time for teenagers to socialize. The bubbling springs pumped life into the resort. The four springs each had a different mineral in the water. Two of the springs were for bathing and two were for drinking. The resort was in operation for all the 28 years that the Presley girls lived in the Tilden community. We believe that John Wallace was one of the musicians that played at the White Springs resort for at least 17 years.

Party at White Springs Resort   Late 1800"s

Itawamba Historical Society

Loving You

Sometime after 1890, John Wallace and Rosella Presley started an affair that lasted for the rest of their lives, and was to have a huge impact on the music world, as we know it today. John and Rosella would have known each other for at least 10 years before they started the affair. Their first child was Jesse Dee McDowell Presley, grandfather of Elvis Presley. John had left the Tilden area for Texas about the time the Presley girls were moving to the Tilden area. When John came back to Mississippi in 1880, he married Elmira McFadden and was to father nine children with her. Rosella Presley appears to have been involved with Tom Hussey until about 1888. January 6, 1889, Tom married his very wealthy distant cousin, Ruth Bottom Lloyd. Ruth moved from Fort Worth, Texas to Richmond, Lee County, Mississippi after the marriage. This ended Tom and Rosella's long time affair.

Rosella moved her children from Tilden to the Eastman Community of Itawamba County after March 1896. She moved next door to Joshua Steele, brother of William Marion Steele, stepfather to Rosella Presley. Jesse Dee Presley was born at Eastman, in Itawamba County, on April 9, 1897. We believe that Rosella had to leave Tilden because she was carrying a married mans child. That would have been something of a scandal at that time. This move by Rosella must have been hard for John Wallace to accept, because he sold the farm at Tilden and on October 1, 1897 and purchased 320 acres on Chubby Creek near the Salem Church in the Fairview Community. He then moved his family from the Tilden area to the north part of

Itawamba County. John made his mark as an X on the deed. The GPS location is 34 degrees 24.932 minutes North 88 degrees 14.063 minutes west. We believe that John moved his family so that he could be near Rosella and his son Jesse Dee McDowell Presley. John and Rosella moved around the north part of Itawamba County, but they were never far apart for the rest of their lives. On the 1900 census, John and his family lived in the Pineville Precinct, Beat 1, in the northern part of Itawamba County. In 1903, John purchased 180 acres in the southern part of Tishomingo County, Mississippi. Tishomingo County is located just north of Itawamba County. They lived just east of the Patterson Chapel Church. The GPS location is 34 degrees 28.234 minutes North 88 degrees 10.152 minutes west. In 1907, the railroad was built through John's 180-acre farm, so by 1909 he moved his family back to the farm on Chubby Creek. On the 1910 census, John and his family are shown to be living in the Copeland Precinct, Beat 1, in the northern part of Itawamba County. On December 1, 1914, John purchased 80 acres of land near Fairview in Itawamba County. The GPS location is 34 degrees 21.802 minutes North 88 degrees18.025 minutes west. This was about 2 miles from where Rosella was living. On the 1920 census, John lived in the Pleasanton Precinct, in the northern part of Itawamba County.

    Rosella Presley, long time girlfriend of John Wallace and mother to nine children, died of cancer on June 30, 1924. At her death, Rosella and John were living about one mile apart on the same dirt road outside of Red Bay, Alabama. John sold the 80 acres near Fairview on October 24, 1927 and moved to Red Bay, Alabama. This is about two miles from where Rosella is buried.

On the 1930 census, John and Elmira are living on Timbs Street, Red Bay, Franklin County, Alabama. Their son, Ausie Homer Wallace, and his wife are living on Grand Avenue, Red Bay, Alabama. Joseph Warren Presley, youngest son of Rosella Presley, is living in Beat 5, Tishomingo County, near Red Bay, Alabama. After Elmira Wallace died on June 6, 1934, John moved to Columbus, Mississippi and lived with his sons until his death on November 17, 1935. John died the same year that Elvis was born. John is buried at the Salem Cemetery in Itawamba County. John is buried about three miles from where he lived when he first moved from the Tilden Community. Rosella and John had followed each other around Itawamba County for over 30 years, and they played an important part in changing the history of music, as we know it today.

Itawamba Historical Society   **Fulton In Itawamba**
County, Mississippi   Late 1800's

Rosella Presley Shortly Before Her Death.

Courtesy Of Patsy Presley Pressnall

Trying To Get To You

    The last weekend in August 2006, Rachel Ann and I stopped at a modest house in the Richmond community that we had passed many times on our way to the Andrews Chapel Cemetery. We were looking for someone in the Rosalinda Presley family line. We knocked on the door and were greeted by Ms. Carthy Presley Derrick, a tall thin elegant 80-year-old lady. She had no idea who we were. We explained what we were trying to do, who we are, and my connections to the Richmond Community. She unlocked the screen door and invited us into her home. Ms. Carthy was the youngest daughter of John A. Jefferson Presley, the oldest son of Rosalinda Presley. Her pictures revealed that she was a beautiful young woman. We thought that she must look a lot like her grandmother, Rosalinda Presley. Ms. Carthy was very interested that we were working on a Presley family tree. She willingly shared her childhood memories, and allowed us to make copies of her family photos. She seemed to enjoy our visit, and we made plans to meet with her again next weekend. Ms. Carthy called her relatives and explained what we were trying to do. She told them that we also wanted to talk to them. On our return visit the next weekend, Ms. Carthy was not at home. Mrs. Donis Deaton, sister and neighbor of Carthy, told us that she had fallen and broke her hip. The next week we would visit with Ms. Carthy at the North Mississippi Medical Center in Tupelo. I remember that she was sitting up with a blanket wrapped around her. We planned to return the next weekend but when we did, we were informed that she had been moved to Corinth, Mississippi. While at Corinth, she had a stroke and on September 23, 2006, she died. Less than a month from our first meeting her, she had passed away. We have tried to continue this work on the Presley tree in her memory.

    Rachel Ann and I started to think that other Elvis fans might also be interested in this Presley and Wallace family information. Some fans may discover that they share a common ancestor with Elvis Presley. That is when we decided to write a book about the Elvis Family Tree and share our experience, and the discoveries we have made. As we continued to accumulate information, the family tree became so large that we could not fit it all into one book. We then decided to first create an extensive web site with the family tree and an accumulation of pictures and documents. This web site is located at "rootsofelvispresley.com". We continue to add names and pictures to the web site every week. If you cannot get enough Elvis Presley, or you think you might be related to him, check out the site. "rootsofelvispresley.com"

    If anyone has a question about the book, the web site, or the family tree, they can e-mail us at aaart101@yahoo.com. We will be glad to try to answer your questions.

So Close Yet So Far

One of the many discoveries we made is that Tupelo had very little to do with the Elvis Presley family tree. All of Elvis Presley's relatives on the Presley, Wallace and Hood lines are from Itawamba County, Mississippi. Most of the important people in the tree are from, or passed through, Itawamba County. Elvis Presley was not born in Tupelo; he was born in East Tupelo. In 1935, these were two separate towns, with two separate governments. More than just a name separated these two towns, and they were much farther apart than the one-mile stretch across the Town Creek bottom. East Tupelo was considered to be on the wrong side of the tracks. East Tupelo was a blue-collar community, with poor people, dirt roads, outdoor toilets, and a reputation for being a rough place to visit. However, East Tupelo did not start out as the wrong side of town. During the civil war, the hills around East Tupelo were selected as a camp for Confederate soldiers. The high hills, with good air and good water were much preferred to the low swampy area where Tupelo was located. After the Civil War Battle of Shiloh, over 30,000 Confederate soldiers and officers were in camp on the hills around East Tupelo. In December of 1864, after the Battle of Nashville, all that remained of the Army of Tennessee walked in the snow over 200 miles from Nashville, Tennessee to camp in the hills around East Tupelo. Many of these men had no shoes, and many died along the way.

Tupelo was established where the railroad crossed the old Indian trail from Pontotoc to Fulton. All of the towns in Lee County are located where Indian trails crossed one of the railroads. The first settlement was called Harrisburg, and was located about two miles west of present Tupelo. When Lee County was formed in 1867, Tupelo was selected as the county seat because it was located near the center of the county.

Before 1900, two families, the Long family from the Shannon area and the Martin family owned the land where East Tupelo is located. On April 1917, Tom A. Hussey gave 63 acres and a house he had purchased from the Martin family to his daughter, Tee Hussey Long, as a present. This house was located on the south side of East Main Street, across the street from the old Saltillo Road. Tom Hussey is one of two brothers that owned the large Hussey farm at Richmond, Lee County, Mississippi. This farm has played an important part in the Presley family tree. Tee Hussey married Sam P. Long who was to become a prominent attorney in Tupelo. How could anyone have known that Tee Long, owner of much of the land where East Tupelo is located, was a first cousin to the children of Martha Jane Presley and Charles Hussey, and the half brother of Noah P. Presley?

The area where East Tupelo is located was first referred to as Longtown and sometimes Longville. This was because of the Long family owning much of the town. William Cullen Snipes and Ruben Marion Martin built the first two homes. Mrs. Wade Hampton Long purchased the Snipes home and farm which was located on the North side of East Main Street. Wade Hampton Long's younger son, Sam Paul Long, married Miss Tee Hussey, daughter of Tom Hussey on July 15, 1915. Tom Hussey purchased the Martin home and 63 acres of land for his daughter and her husband. The Martin home was on the South side of East Main Street. Because this early settlement was one mile east of Tupelo, Mississippi, it was referred to as East Tupelo as early as 1921, but the only charter that has been found dates February 22, 1934. The first elected mayor of East Tupelo was William R. Mitchell. Elvis's great uncle Noah P. Presley served as mayor from January 7, 1936 to January 1938. It was under the leadership of Noah P. Presley that East Tupelo made great strides in improving its physical facilities. A community water system and sewer system became operational during the term of Noah P. Presley. No longer did residents of East Tupelo have to use outdoor toilets or to draw their water from wells. A dress factory known as the Tillie Murphy Factory was started at 201 South Canal Street in East Tupelo in 1911. Mr. Post opened the factory for Jeanie Murphy Brown of Macon, Missouri. In 1930, Mrs. Chester Brown managed the factory and the assistant manager was her husband. This factory provided regular employment for local women and was the reason many of the first families moved to East Tupelo. The factory was moved to Red Bay, Alabama in 1937 where the town of Red Bay built a factory for Mrs. Chester Brown. After the factory moved, many of the women moved over and worked at the garment factory in South Tupelo.

   Before East Tupelo was a chartered town, it was the location of a consolidated school system for the east part of Lee County. On September 2, 1925, G. W. Crider presented a petition to the Lee County School Board to build a school that would educate the students of the Priceville, Briar Ridge, Oak Hill and East Tupelo. The school was built one block south of the Bankhead Highway on land that had at one time belonged to Tom Hussey. Elvis would have attended this school, starting in the third grade. On October 28, 1946, East Tupelo Consolidated School was merged with the Tupelo City School system and the name was changed to Lawhon in honor of Mr. Ross Lawhon.

Tom A. Hussey built the first movie theater in Lee County on the corner of Main Street and Lake Street in East Tupelo. This was on Sam and Tee Long's property. People would come from all over the area to see a real moving picture show. We believe that Tom Hussey would have liked the old silent western movies. This building later became a bowling alley and then a nightclub known as The Tavern. By late 1934, The Tavern had been shut down and the building turned into the Assembly of God Church.

In the early 1930's, a public dance hall was opened in East Tupelo. Several other nightspots were opened after that. One of the first dance halls was the Owl's Roost, owned and operated by Chester F. Brown, the assistant manager of the Tillie Murphy dress factory. This favorite gathering place was located just off East Main Street as you turn onto Highway 6. Another dance spot was called Melrose. It was located at the southeast corner of Old highway 78 and Feemster's Lake Road. The open-air dance floor extended over Feemster Lake.

On the West side of Highway 6 was a group of buildings that made the local churchwomen very unhappy. East Tupelo, like all of Lee County, always had its share of bootleggers. Bootleggers are people who sold illegal alcohol. This is how East Tupelo got its reputation as a rough and lawless place. Not

The Roots of Elvis

because of the families living there, but because of the outside element the nightclubs attracted.

On September 30, 1946, a special election was held to determine if East Tupelo would merge with Tupelo. The qualified voters of East Tupelo voted 110 to 77 to merge with Tupelo, hoping to be accepted, and to clean up its reputation. This hoped for acceptance did not happen. Not much has changed over the years except the name. Now it is called Presley Heights, but is still sometimes treated as the wrong side of the tracks. Because of its reputation, there was a stigma about being from East Tupelo that we think Elvis was never able to overcome. Some Tupelo citizens in the 1950s had a hard time accepting the success of a poor boy from East Tupelo whose father had been to prison. They could not believe that rock and roll was here to stay and Elvis Presley was the King.

One Of The Nightclubs In East Tupelo   Courtesy of The Oren Dunn Museum, Tupelo

Marshall Brown, Vona Mae Presley Brown, J. P. Brown, And Joyce Brown   Courtesy Of Freddy Brown

Marshall and Vona Mae Brown are the couple that drove Gladys and Vernon to Pontotoc, Mississippi to get their marriage license, and back to Verona, Mississippi to be married by Justice of the Peace Robert Emmitt Kelly. They also provided the money to pay for the marriage license.

The Green, Green Grass of Home

This Presley family story began with the birth of two sisters in Itawamba County, Mississippi, during the War for Southern Independence. All of the local Presley family related to Elvis can be traced back to these two women and most of the roots of Elvis are in the red hills of Itawamba County, Mississippi. Any close relatives of Elvis Presley on the Smith or Presley sides will have to have family from or close to Itawamba County. Martha Jane Wesson and Dunnan Presley were married in Itawamba County on August 15, 1861. This was less than a year before the start of the war that was to have such a large impact on the lives of these two girls, and all of the Southern people. Martha Jane Wesson was the daughter of Edward Clanton Wesson and Emily Millie Bowen. In 1860, Martha Jane was living with her parents and sister, Emma, at Tremont, Itawamba County, Mississippi. Dunnan Presley was the son of Dunnan and Mary Catherine Presley. This may have been the second marriage for Dunnan Presley, and was the first marriage for Martha Jane Wesson. Dunnan had a wife and five children living in Tennessee in 1861. Dunnan began living with Elizabeth Hooper Harrison in 1845, and fathered her five children. We have not found a marriage license for the couple. In 1860, Elizabeth is living with her mother at Sweet Water, Monroe County, Tennessee. We do not know why Dunnan Presley was in Itawamba County. He may have received land there as payment for his service in the war with Mexico. He left Tennessee sometime after 1854, and we have not found him on the 1860 census for any state.

The Roots of Elvis

The first daughter of Dunnan and Martha Jane Wesson Presley, Rosella Elizabeth Presley, was born on February 16, 1861. This date is taken from her tombstone. If this date is correct, then Rosella would have been born six months before the marriage of her parents. The 1870 census, which was taken in June 1870, shows Rosella as 7 years old. The 1880 census, which was taken in June, 1880, shows Rosella as 17 years old. This would indicate that the tombstone is incorrect, and she was born in 1863, not 1861. Rosella is of special interest to us because she is the great grandmother of Elvis Presley. The second daughter Rosalinda (Mary Jane) Presley was born December 25, 1863. This date is taken from funeral home records based on information provided by family members. The 1870 census shows Rosalinda as 5 years old. The 1880 census shows Rosalinda as 15 years old. This would indicate that she was born in 1864, not 1863. Many times tombstones were erected years after the death, and the family members did not remember the correct dates. We have found many errors on tombstones and on census records. Dunnan Presley had served as a soldier under General Winfield Scott in the United States war with Mexico. We believe that the names Rosella and Rosalinda came from names of women Dunnan knew in Mexico.

Dunnan Presley was a soldier in the Confederate Army in the War for Southern Independence. Much has been made of the fact that Dunnan was a member of several different military units and that he was listed for a time as a deserter. It may be that neither is an indication of his loyalty to the Southern cause. Dunnan was about 35 years old when the war started. Older men joined local military units, which were much like today's

National Guard. The men in these military units would have lived at home some of the time. These units were used as they were needed, and the unit designation may have changed several times. This could make it appear that he had joined different units, when he had not. Dunnan first joined Company A, Brown's Company, Davenport's Battalion, Mississippi State Cavalry. Dunnan joined as a private. Next Dunnan served as a corporal in Ham's Regiment of Mississippi Cavalry. This unit later became Ashcraft's 11th Regiment of Mississippi Cavalry. My great grandfather, William Sylvester Sheffield, served in the 11th Cavalry Regiment with Dunnan Presley. William Sheffield joined the cavalry when he was just 14 years of age. All of the units that Dunnan served in were from Itawamba County, Mississippi. For the last part of 1863, all of 1864, and the first part of 1865, General Nathan Bedford Forrest was the commander of the all armed forces in North Mississippi. General Forrest had a headquarters camp and supply depot established at Verona, Mississippi. General Forrest's reputation was such that it is very unlikely that Dunnan, or any other soldier, would have deserted his command and lived to tell the story. What is a fact is that sometime after the birth of Rosalinda, Dunnan Presley left Mississippi and never returned. In the spring of 1865, General Forrest's command was ordered to Selma, Alabama and by April 1865, the war was over. We have no evidence that Dunnan ever returned to Itawamba County after the war ended. The stories about the two sisters coming home from church to find that Dunnan had deserted them are probably just family stories told to them by their grandmother. The girls were less than three years old at the time. We doubt that they would have remembered this event.

The Roots of Elvis

On September 9, 1868, Martha Jane Wesson Presley married William Marion Steele. The name Martha Jane used on the marriage license is Mrs. M. J. Wesson. She was using her maiden name when she married William Steele. Martha Jane may have believed Dunnan was killed in Alabama in the Selma campaign or she may have known that Dunnan had deserted his family. This was the second time Dunnan had run off leaving his children behind. Because so many young men did not survive the war, the men who did survive had their choice of the young women they could marry. Very old men were marrying very young women. Martha Jane must have been a very pretty woman, because she was about 28 years old and already had two children when she married William Steele. We have not found Martha Jane, her sister Emma, or Martha's parents on any 1870 census.

William Marion Steele was born about 1839 in North Carolina or Georgia. We have found both states reported as states of his birth on different census records. Georgia is the state most often reported. William's family moved from North Carolina into Georgia and then to Alabama. They moved into Itawamba County, Mississippi about 1852. William and his brother Joshua T. Steele joined and served in Company G, 43rd Regiment, Mississippi Infantry in the War. After the War, William Steele owned a farm south of Fulton in the Union Grove community of Itawamba County. Martha Jane had relatives on the Bowen side living in the Union Grove area of Itawamba County. Martha Jane and William had one daughter, Josephine, who was listed as two years old on the 1870 census. Martha Jane either died or abandoned her daughters to be cared for by

William Steele before 1870. We believe Martha Jane died before the 1870 census, and we assume that it might have been from complications of childbirth. This was one of the main causes of death for young women in the 19th century. The child Josephine Steele does not appear on any record after the 1870 census, and we assume that she died as a child. No tombstone has been located for Martha Jane or her daughter, Josephine. We believe they may be buried in unmarked graves in the Union Grove Cemetery at Tilden, Itawamba County, Mississippi.

On the 1870 census, the two Presley sisters were living at Tilden with their stepfather, William Marion Steele. On September 14, 1871, William Steele married Sarah Brown, daughter of J. William Brown and Sarah Kitchens. This would indicate that William knew that Martha Jane was dead. We think that as the sisters got older William's wife may have wanted the young girls out of the house. Sometimes young girls can be a distraction. Millie Bowen Wesson, the mother of Martha Jane Wesson Presley and grandmother of the 2 Presley sisters, stepped in to help with the care of her two granddaughters. On February 17, 1875, William Steele sold 80 acres of land and a place for them to live on the White Springs road in what is now the Tilden community in the southern part of Itawamba County, to Millie Bowen Wesson. The GPS location for the cabin is 34 degrees 10.555 minutes North 88 degrees 22.097 minutes west. At that time, the community was known as Union Grove. The log cabin the Presley sisters lived in was two miles down a dirt road and was one half mile from the home of William Steele. We know very little about the life of these girls. We do know that two young girls and a grandmother would have required some assistance to survive. The 1890 Federal census was destroyed and information that would have been very helpful has been lost. We do know that grandmother, Millie Bowen Wesson, had relatives living in the community, so they did not grow up alone. The girls had a cousin named Rosalinda, born in 1864 and living in the same community. There were at least two local churches but no school in the community. There was a local doctor and a ferry across the Tombigbee River a few miles north of Tilden. The White Springs Resort would have played an important role in the lives of these two sisters.

The results of the War for Southern Independence were that the South was left a devastated country, and what natural resources survived the war, were being shipped north. Another result was that so many young men had been killed, maimed and destroyed mentally, that there were few men for young women to marry. Many times women married men as much as 40 years older than themselves. Surviving day to day was very hard for Southern women after the war. There is no way these women can be or should be judged by today's standards. They did not have the benefits of social security, welfare, food stamps, Medicare, minimum wage, or any other of today' social programs. Much of the time that the Presley girls were growing up, Mississippi and much of the South was suffering under forced reconstruction. The Federal government was trying to make life as hard as possible for the Southern people. Surviving day to day was a constant problem.

The 1880 census is the last time that the name Rosalinda Presley is found on any record. She appears on later census records as Mary Jane, Rose Mary and Rosa Presley. We do know that the girl's grandmother, Millie Bowen Wesson, sold her land on the White Springs road, back to William Marion Steele on March 23, 1896. Millie may have died around that time, but no tombstone for Millie has been located, and she does not appear on the 1900 census. We believe Millie may be buried with her granddaughter, Martha Jane Presley Hussey at Andrews Chapel Cemetery north of Richmond in Lee County.

No record has been found that either of the Presley sisters ever married. This may have been due to the lack of young men to marry, and the choice to not marry someone much older than them. The two girls were to give birth to fourteen children that survived. All of these children took the Presley name, but all had fathers with another name. At that time, women worked in the home and fields, and often did not travel out of the local community. They tended to marry men they went to church with, or worked in the fields with, met at the local social events, or many times, they married cousins. We do not think that the sisters did not want to be married; they just did what they had to do to survive. It appears that the sisters had relationships with men who could help them and their children survive. None of the family members we interviewed could tell us who were the fathers of the fourteen children, but it is unreasonable to think the children did not know who was coming to visit their mother. They lived in a small community and in a small cabin; they would have known the men who were friends with their mother. We believe that the children knew who their fathers were, and that the mothers sometimes left clues to the fathers in the names they gave their children.

The Roots of Elvis

Rosella Presley's Milk Pitcher

Rosella Presley's Necklace

These Items Courtesy Of Patsy Presley Pressnall

The Roots of Elvis

We have only found one picture of Rosella and no picture of Mary Jane. The picture of Rosella was made when she was about 60 years old. This was shortly before her death. Both of these sisters must have been very pretty women. We have found pictures of their granddaughters, and they are very pretty girls.

The 1880 census did not show any children in the home with the two Presley sisters, but the 1900 census indicates that both of the girls were pregnant before 1880. Rosella's oldest son, Walter Presley, was born on December 19, 1878. Mary Jane's oldest daughter, Martha Jane Presley, was born in 1879. Martha Jane Presley was to marry Charles Christopher Hussey, the younger of the two Hussey brothers and one of the wealthiest men in Lee County, Mississippi. We do not know where these two babies were when the 1880 census taker came around in 1880.

We have found conflicting dates of birth for some of the members of this family tree. The family records would say one date, the census would say another date, the tombstone would say another date, and the draft registration records would say another date. We have used the draft registration dates first because the individual recorded them and he should know his birthday. Next, we would use the family records because a family member recorded them. Next, we used the tombstone record and then the census record. On the census, sometimes the individual lied about their age, or did not remember. On the tombstone, many times the surviving family did not remember the date of birth, and sometimes the company creating the tombstone would make a mistake.

Rosella's son Noah Presley was born August 29, 1887 and Mary Jane's son John A. Jefferson Presley was born June 28, 1887. The two boys were born two months apart and we believe they had the same father. The two boys were first cousins, but they were raised as brothers in the small cabin on the White Springs road in Itawamba County. After March 1896, Rosella Presley took her family of three children and moved next door to Joshua Steele, brother of William Marion Steele, in the Eastman Community of Itawamba County, three miles northeast of Fulton, Mississippi. Millie Bowen Wesson had sold her land back to William Marion Steele, and we do not find her on any record after 1896. It appears that William Steele was still trying to help take care of his stepdaughters and their children.

It was here between the Eastman and Clay Community of Itawamba County that Jesse Dee McDowell Presley is born on April 9, 1896. The GPS location is 34 degrees 18.463 minutes North 88 degrees 17.315 minutes west. Jesse Dee McDowell Presley is of special interest because he is the grandfather of Elvis Presley. On the 1900 census, Rosella Presley is living in the Eastman Community northeast of Fulton in Itawamba County with five of her children. Her neighbors are J. M. Pierce on one side and Joshua Steele on the other side. Joshua Steele is the brother of William Marion Steele. The 1910 census shows that Walter Presley, oldest son of Rosella, had moved back to the Tilden community and was living next door to William Marion Steele. All of William Marion Steele's children were living around him. We believe that William Marion Steele is the father of Walter Presley. When Walter left his mother's house, he went to live next door to William Marion Steele, his father.

Walter Presley and Marion Pink Steele married sisters. When the Steele family sold some timber rights in the 1920's, and all of William's Steele's children were required to sign the deed. Walter Presley was also required to sign the deed. The Steele family knew Walter was William's son. Walter Presley's youngest daughter told us that the only time Walter Presley owned his own home was when he lived next door to William Steele. On the 1920 census of Itawamba County, Walter is living in the Tilden Community between Marion Pink Steele and Vollie Joseph Steele. The census taker made a mistake on recording the results of his work by adding a dash after Vollie Joseph Steele's name, making some researchers to conclude that the name was Vollie Joseph Steele Presley.

We think Rosella left Tilden and moved to the north part of Itawamba County because she was pregnant and she needed help with her children. We believe that there may have been something of a scandal at Tilden because Rosella was pregnant with John Wallace's child, and John was a married man. Joshua Steele's wife, Melvina Raper Steele, died about 1902. We have found errors in her date of death. The tombstone shows a date of 1895, and other records show 1892. These records cannot be correct because she is still alive in 1900. Melvina Raper Steele is shown on the 1900 census as the wife of Joshua Steele. She had to have died between 1900 and 1903. After her death, Joshua was alone with a house and farm to take care of. The Steele family had been involved with the Presley girls for over thirty years because William Steele was their stepfather. This move to the Joshua Steele farm was a good deal for Rosella and her family, but did not make John Wallace, the father of Jesse

Dee Presley very happy. Rosella Presley and her family lived next door to Joshua Steele for about 10 years. Rosella's oldest daughter, Minnie Fee "Docia" Presley, was married to Joshua Steele on August 2, 1903. Joshua was much older than Docia. She was to become the last surviving widow of a Confederate soldier in the state of Mississippi.

Doshie, Noah, Christine, Odis, Cal, Robbie, Joseph, Minnie Mae, Delma, and Monervia at Presley Family Reunion. Courtesy Of Patsy Presley Pressnall

The 1910 census shows Rosella living in the Clay Community, on Cobb Stump Road. Her son Noah P. Presley is listed as the head of household. Rosella is living there with six of her children. All the children living with her listed their father as born in Mississippi. This is important because there were no Presley men born in Mississippi living in Itawamba County, except the sons of Rosella Presley. All of these children had fathers with names other than Presley. Rosella's oldest son Walter and oldest daughter Docia have married and the second daughter Essie has died. We have not found a tombstone for Essie, but we believe she is buried at the Joshua Steele family cemetery. The Presleys are the neighbors of several of the Hood families at this time. Like many families in Mississippi during that time, Rosella sharecropped to make a living and had to move many times. The 1920 census shows Rosella living on the Bankhead Highway near Stones Cross Roads in Itawamba County. Stones Cross Roads is near the present community of Tremont in Itawamba County. On the 1920 census, Rosella is listed as the head of household and is living with her daughter Robbie and her son Joseph Warren Presley. Rosella's son Mack Presley, died about 1917 or 1918, and is buried in an unmarked grave at Mount Pleasant Cemetery, on Old Highway 78 east of Tremont, Mississippi near the Alabama State line. Noah Presley has taken his family and moved to East Tupelo in Lee County. Jesse Dee Presley is in the Army or the National Guard and will soon take his family and move to East Tupelo in Lee County. We do not know why Rosella did not move to East Tupelo with her sons, but we believe she stayed in Itawamba County because John Wallace was in Itawamba County.

By 1924, daughter Robbie Presley was married to Odis Stacy, and Rosella's youngest son, Joseph Warren Presley was living with and taking care of his mother. This was not an easy job for a seventeen-year-old young man. At this time, they were living in a small house with no front porch in Northeast Itawamba County, neat the Mississippi, Alabama state line. The GPS location is 34 degrees 26.481 minutes North 88 degrees 10.784 minutes west. John Wallace was living a few miles from Rosella at this time. Rosella Elizabeth Presley died of cancer in Itawamba County, just outside of Red Bay, Alabama on July 30, 1924. A neighbor, George Washington Davis, reported her death. The Davis family is related to Elvis on Minnie Mae Hood's side of the family. Rosella is buried at Ridge Cemetery in the northeast part of Itawamba County. Initially, there was a homemade marker on her grave that said "Our Mother". Later it was replaced with a granite marker. Based on census records, we believe the date on the marker (1861) is incorrect. The GPS location is 34 degrees 27.008 minutes North 88 degrees 10.794 minutes west. Epitaphs read "Our Mother" and "Gone but not forgotten". Family members say that an unmarked burial space near Rosella is the grave of Robbie Presley Stacey's child, which would be the grandchild of Rosella.

Rosella was a simple, uneducated, hardworking woman, who cared for her family and survived as best she could. She survived the War for Southern Independence, the abandonment of her father, the death of her mother and grandmother, and the death of two of her children. She lived through a time of rebuilding in the South that made living very hard for poor southern families. Had Mississippi been treated as well as the countries the United States defeated in WWI and WWII, Mississippi would be a wealthy state today.

Rosella's children are Walter G. Presley born December 19, 1878, Essie Presley, Minnie Fee Docia Presley born June 22, 1886, Noah P. Presley born August 29, 1887, Jesse Dee McDowell Presley born April 9, 1896, and Calhoun Presley born May 9, 1898, Mack Presley born in 1900, Robbie Presley born March 1, 1903, and Joseph Warren Presley born January 6, 1907

**Joseph And Delma Presley Wedding Photo
Courtesy Of Patsy Presley Pressnall**

The Roots of Elvis

Joseph And Delma Presley Summer of 1925 Standing in A Cotton Field

The Roots of Elvis

Robbie, Haskell, Delma, Bytha, Joseph, And Flavis At Gravesite Of Rosella Presley In Itawamba County At Ridge Cemetery   Courtesy Of Patsy Presley Pressnall

The Roots of Elvis

Calhoun Presley And Family about 1930 Shortly Before His Wife Dies   Picture Was Made In Arkansas Courtesy Of Freddy Brown

The Roots of Elvis

**Presley Family Gathering Easter 1951 In Itawamba County
Courtesy Of Patsy Presley Pressnall**

The Roots of Elvis

Walter Presley And Samantha Presley At Their Home Near White Springs About 1920   Courtesy of Nannie Presley

Minnie Mae Hood Presley

The Roots of Elvis

**John A. Jefferson Presley And Minnie Raper Presley
Known As Big John, He Was The Oldest Son Of Mary Jane
Rosalinda Presley and First Cousin Of Noah Presley
Courtesy Of Carthy Presley**

Little Sister

The story of the other sister, Rosalinda has never been told, and she was not an easy person to find. In 1870, Rosalinda was living with her sister and stepfather in the Union Grove area of Itawamba County. In 1880, Rosalinda was living with her sister and grandmother down a dirt road in the Union Grove community, six miles south of Fulton in Itawamba County. Before 1880, Rosalinda was pregnant with her first child Martha Jane Presley. Records indicate that she may have already given birth, but there is no child listed in the household on the 1880 census. We do know that by 1900 Rosalinda has six children. We think she may have left Tilden about 1896 when her grandmother, Millie Wesson, sold her land back to William Marion Steele. On the 1900 census, Rosalinda is living at Central Grove in Monroe, County, Mississippi, with five of her children, and is using the name Mary Jane Presley. We believe that Mary Jane is her correct name, and that Rosalinda was a nickname. Her oldest child, Martha Jane Presley is living with Charles Christopher Hussey. Charley Hussey was born at Richmond in Lee County on February 14, 1866. Charles was about the same age as two Presley sisters. Charles Hussey was a wealthy, good-looking, educated, businessman. About 1900 Charles had a telegraph line run from Tupelo to Richmond so that he could play the stock market. That was a distance of about fifteen miles. Charles was also on the board of directors of Peoples Bank and Trust Company. Brothers Charles and Tom Hussey will inherit the Hussey Farm, which contained several thousand acres of farmland. This farm will play an important part in the search for Elvis Presley's family tree. The match of Martha Jane Presley from Tilden and Charles C. Hussey from Richmond was a real life Cinderella and the handsome prince story.

Rosalinda's other children are Ofelia born in October, 1883, John A. Jefferson Presley born June 28, 1887, Duskey Presley born May 1888, William Buchanan (Buck) Presley born January 3, 1893, and Thomas Eleanach (Canan) Presley born February 28, 1899. John A. Presley and Noah P. Presley were first cousins, but were raised as brothers in the same cabin on White Springs Road at Tilden, Itawamba County, Mississippi. Mary Jane and all of her children are buried at the Andrews Chapel Cemetery north of Richmond, Lee County, Mississippi.

The Reed family that was to become so important to the garment industry in Tupelo and northeast Mississippi was living in the Tilden area of Itawamba County the same time as the Presley sisters. The Reed family and the Presley family lived near each other and would have known each other for years. Dr. Madison L. Reed may have helped with the birth of Rosella and Rosalinda's children. Rosalinda's third child was named Duskey Presley. We believe she was named after the wife of Dr. Madison Reed; Loduska Farrar Reed. Dr. Madison Reed and his son Robert W. Reed purchased a store in Tilden about 1900. Robert W. Reed worked there until about 1907 when the J. J. Rogers family convinced him to move his business to Tupelo and continue his career there. The Reed family that was to become leaders in the economic and political development of Tupelo, and the Presley family that was to become famous all over the music world, all came from the Tilden Community in

Itawamba County, Mississippi.

The 1910 census was a real mystery. We found Mary Jane Presley living in Beat 3, Chickasaw County, Mississippi. Her name on the census is Rose Mary, but it was recorded in error by the census taker as Mary Ross. It is hard to find the name Presley when it is listed as Ross. On this census, Mary Jane Presley is the head of household and four of her children and three grandchildren are living with her. Her oldest son John is married to Minnie Raper and is living in Richmond, Lee County, Mississippi. Her oldest daughter Martha Jane Presley Hussey is counted in her mother's household in Chickasaw County, on April 27, 1910. She is also counted in the household of her husband Charles C. Hussey at Richmond on May 5, 1910, along with six of her children. We think Martha Jane must have been visiting her mother when the census taker came by. Other members of Mary Jane Presley's household are daughter, Ofelia, and Ofelia's two sons, John born November 3, 1903, and Floyd born in 1905. Duskey Presley and her son, William David (Verdie) Pendergast, are also living in the house. William David was born August 21, 1908. His father, William Pendergast, is living two houses away with the family of John Riley. Mary Jane's sons William Buchanan (Buck) Presley and Thomas Eleanach (Canan) Presley are also listed as living in the household.

On the 1920 census, Mary Jane Presley is living outside of Verona, Mississippi with her youngest son Thomas Eleanach Presley. Thomas is married to Effie F. Curry, daughter of George L. and Martha C. Curry. The two families are next-door neighbors. Mary Jane's son, William Buck Presley is married to Birdy Curry, sister of Effie Curry and is living in the Richmond community. The two brothers were married to two sisters.

On the 1930 census, Mary Jane Presley is living at Richmond, Mississippi with her oldest daughter, Martha Jane Presley Hussey. After Charles C. Hussey died in 1915, Martha Jane married her brother in law, William Pendergast. William had been married to Duskey Presley, sister of Martha Jane. In the same household is William David Pendergast, son of William and Duskey, and Mary and Hazel Hussey daughters of Charles C. and Martha Jane Presley Hussey.

Mary Jane (Rosalinda) Presley died November 16, 1932 in Richmond, Mississippi. The younger of the two Presley sisters is buried at Andrews Chapel Cemetery two miles north of Richmond. There are no dates of birth or death on her tombstone. Her tombstone was placed there several years after her death and family members were unsure of the dates of birth and death. This tombstone is located about 15 feet from my grandparents. I had been walking past her grave all of my life and did not know whom she was. Andrews Chapel Cemetery is important to the Elvis story because of the great number of relatives on both sides of the Elvis Presley tree that are at rest there. Mary Jane Presley, all six of her children and most of her grandchildren are buried at Andrews Chapel Cemetery in Lee County, Mississippi. There is a good reason that all of that family was living at Richmond, Mississippi.

One of the daughters of Dunnan Presley and Martha Jane

Wesson is buried at Ridge Cemetery in the northern part of Itawamba County; the other is buried at Andrews Chapel Cemetery in Lee County, Mississippi. They lived and survived hard times in rural Mississippi. Rosella had eight, children that survived; Mary Jane had six children that survived. This group of 14 children is an interesting and colorful group and has been a challenge to research. We have found many clues as to who the fathers of these children are, and we believe that with the help of DNA testing we can, after 120 years, prove some of the fathers.

Tombstone Of Mary Jane "Rosalinda" Presley

The Roots of Elvis

Our search for the fathers of the Presley children has led in some unexpected directions. One of the most unexpected for me was the Richmond area of Lee County. The history of old Richmond was something I had worked on while at school at Mississippi State University. The Andrews Chapel cemetery is the resting place of many of my family, and many people related to Elvis Presley. Some of these families, such as the Smith, Mansell, Presley, Hussey, and Tackett, are important to the Elvis Presley story.

Last House Standing At The Old Town Of Richmond, Mississippi   Picture Was Made In 1964 By Julian Riley

Burt Home In Richmond, Mississippi About 1880

Carthy Presley, Granddaughter Of Mary Jane Presley

The Roots of Elvis

**Mable Hussey, Granddaughter Of Mary Jane Presley
Courtesy Of Thelma Riley Shumpert**

Receipt For Rosalinda Presley's Casket

I'm Movin' On

One big question in our minds from the beginning of the research has been, why East Tupelo? Why was the Presley family living in East Tupelo? Why did two brothers who were born and raised in Itawamba County move to East Tupelo in Lee County? Without this move, Vernon would not have been there to meet Gladys Smith and there would be no Elvis Presley. Many small pieces have fallen into place, and we now think we know why the Presleys were living in East Tupelo.

Noah P. Presley, great uncle of Elvis Presley, made the first move to East Tupelo. The 1910 census shows that Noah is living in the Clay Community of Itawamba County. He is listed as the head of household of the family that included his mother, Rosella, and four of his siblings. His youngest brother, Joseph Warren Presley, is not shown on the 1910 census. We do not know where Joseph is at that time or why he was not counted. He was born in 1907 and should have been counted. On July 4, 1910, Noah married Susan Griffin. She was listed as Miss Susan Griffin on the marriage license, but she had three sons before she married Noah. The sons are Sumpter Griffin, James Whitford Griffin, and Eackford Griffin. Noah took these three boys into his home and raised them as his own children. Whitford (Whit) and Eackford (Eack) took the Presley name, but Sumpter (Sump) kept the last name of Griffin. Descendents of these three men considered Noah Presley as their grandfather. During the years of 1912 and 1918, Noah and Susan would have six children. They were Vona Mae, Sedera, Ruble, Goble, and a set of fraternal twins, Sales and Gordon. Vona Mae and Sales would later play a part in the Elvis Presley story. The 1920 census indicates that most of the boys have a nickname, and we believe Sales was also a nickname for the given name, Persell. Noah Presley registered for the WWI draft on June 5, 1917 at Wiginton's store, Itawamba County. He gave his year of birth as 1887, and we believe this year to be correct because he would have had no reason to lie to US Army at that time, he would have known when he was born. Noah recorded his employment as, farmer. He was described as tall, medium build, dark blue eyes, and black hair. Noah is 30 years old and is responsible for a large family that includes his mother, his siblings, and his wife, children, and stepchildren. On November 5, 1917, Noah purchased a farm of 110 acres from William Townley for $600. This farm was located about two miles south of Tremont in Itawamba County. Noah then packed up his rather large family and moved them almost 40 miles to East Tupelo in Lee County, Mississippi. On November 19, 1918, Noah sold the same

110-acre farm to C. C. Guess for $500.00. Why would a responsible man leave his mother and siblings behind, move his family to a county where he has no relatives, and sell his farm for less than he paid for it one year earlier? The 1920 federal census shows Noah Presley and his family living on the Old Saltillo Road in East Tupelo. How and why did he move to East Tupelo from Itawamba County? This is important to the Elvis story because Jesse Dee Presley followed his brother Noah Presley to East Tupelo about 1924 and the stage is set for Vernon Presley and Gladys Smith to meet each other in 1933.

We have tried to think of all the reasons Noah might have had to make this move from Itawamba County to East Tupelo. He had no family or connections in Lee County that we knew of. He did not stay on his new farm long enough to make a crop. His younger brother, Mack Presley had died and is buried east of Tremont, Mississippi. His mother, Rosella, was left behind with the younger siblings, Robbie and Joe.

The Roots of Elvis

There was a flu epidemic worldwide at the time, but East Tupelo would be no safer from flu than Itawamba County. We were having a hard time thinking of a reasonable reason for the move that fit with Noah's responsible character. Then our research with Patsy Presley Pressnall, daughter of Joe Presley the younger brother of Noah, revealed a picture of Jesse Dee Presley in a World War I military uniform. This was the first indication we had that Jesse Dee Presley may have been drafted. This is the earliest picture we have found of Jesse Dee Presley. Jesse either was drafted or had joined the Mississippi National Guard. When seeing this picture, I realized that Noah was worried that he might be drafted. With all the family members dependent on him, Noah being drafted would have been a disaster for the Presley family. This would have been a legitimate worry for men in 1918, and would have been a reason to make the move from Itawamba County. But how would moving from Itawamba County to Lee County keep Noah from being drafted? Noah would have to know someone with influence with the draft board in Lee County. Noah Presley knew just such a man. Tom Hussey, the older of the two Hussey brothers that owned the large Hussey farm, had the political and financial influence to keep the necessary farm labor out of the military. We know that Noah Presley knew Tom Hussey, because Tom's younger brother Charles C. Hussey had married Noah's first cousin, Martha Jane Presley. Tom Hussey had just purchased 60 acres in East Tupelo for his daughter, Tee Hussey Long, and her husband. When Noah Presley moves to East Tupelo, he lives just across the road from Tee Hussey Long. We believe that Noah's connection to Tom Hussey helped him in many other ways, but without this move to East Tupelo by Noah Presley,

The Roots of Elvis

there would not have been an Elvis Presley.

On December 07, 1939, Noah Presley's wife, Susan Griffin Presley died at her home in East Tupelo. . She was buried beside her daughter Sedera Presley, at the Priceville Cemetery. On December 06, 1940, Noah marries Mrs. Christine Houston Roberts. She was divorced from Edgar Roberts. She had two children, Bobby and Mary Jo Roberts. On the marriage application, Noah states that his father's name is Tom Presley, and his mother is Mrs. Tom Presley. We know that Noah's mother is Rosella Presley; we know Rosella never married, so who is this Tom Presley? Jessie Dee Presley would later record that his father was John Presley. There was no John Presley and there was no Tom Presley, but there was a John Wallace and there was a Tom Hussey and a Tom Morris.

Noah Presley As Town Marshall In East Tupelo

Noah Presley Standing In Front Of His Grocery Store At 292 East Main Street In East Tupelo   Noah Is Standing By His Dodge School Bus   The same Bus He Used To Take Gladys To Visit Vernon In Prison
Pictures Of Noah Courtesy Of Norma Presley

The Roots of Elvis

We have found early pictures of many of the Presley families, but not Jesse Dee Presley family. We have found pictures of many family reunions, but Jesse Dee is never in any of them. Maybe he did not want to be with his family, or maybe they did not want to be with him. Jesse has been described as very good looking, hard drinking, and a hard working man. He has also been described as very selfish and self-centered. We believe these descriptions to be true. Jesse was not a good father figure for his family or his grandson, Elvis.

We know that Jesse Dee Presley was born on the Joshua Steele farm in the Eastman community of Itawamba County on April 9, 1897. His full name has been recorded as Jesse Dee "McClowell" Presley. We believe that is a mistake made on early records. There was no McClowell in Itawamba County, Mississippi. Rosella could not read or write. We do not believe she was making up names. Writing McDowell with a small d could make it appear as a cl. This error would have been repeated over and over for all his life. We do not know how much education Jesse may have had, but we know as a child he would have moved often and would have worked hard to help support the family. Rosella's family never owned a home, and they were always living with the help of others.

Jesse Dee registered for the World War I draft on June 5, 1918 giving his address as Route 2 Fulton, Itawamba County, Mississippi. That GPS location is 24 degrees 20.823 minutes North 88 degrees 20.828 minutes west. This is where Vernon Elvis Presley is born on April 10, 1916. The draft registration described Jesse Dee as tall, slender build with blue eyes and black hair. Jesse signed his name as J. D. Presley, so we know he could read and write. We assume Jesse Dee was drafted or joined the National Guard because we have found a picture of Jesse in a military uniform. His draft registration gives his year of birth as 1897; however, his marriage license to Vera and his death certificate give his year of birth as 1896. The picture that we found is of brothers Jesse Dee, Mack, and Calhoun Presley. The picture would have been made between 1917 and 1920.

Jesse Dee Presley and Minnie Mae Hood had five children. Vester Lee Presley was born September 11, 1914 in Itawamba County. Vernon Elvis Presley was born April 10, 1916, in Itawamba County. Delta Mae Presley was born June 19, 1919 in Itawamba County. Gladys Earline Presley was born June 19, 1923. Nashville Lorene Presley was born December 14, 1925. We are not sure if Nashville was born in Itawamba County or Lee County. We have not found a marriage license for Jesse Dee Presley and Minnie Mae Hood. We have looked in Itawamba County and every county in Mississippi and Alabama that touched Itawamba County. The two only lived a few miles from the Courthouse in Fulton, Itawamba County, so they could have gone there for the marriage license, but evidently did not.

Jesse Dee moved his family to East Tupelo sometime about 1924. We believe that Jesse followed his brother, Noah P. Presley, to East Tupelo after Jesse was discharged from the military. On March 29, 1924, Jesse Dee purchased property in Lee County from S. H. Weil for $1100.00. We believe this is when Jesse Dee first moves his family to Lee County. Jesse Dee purchased property on Old Saltillo Road in East Tupelo from Hazzie and Addie Long on January 10, 1927. Hazzie Long was the brother of Sam P. Long who married Tee Hussey. The note for the property was paid off and was canceled on April 17, 1934 by Mrs. Hazzie Long. Jesse owned his home, something Vernon was only able to do for about one year in his life, until Elvis purchased him a house in Memphis. Jesse Dee lived and raised his family in East Tupelo until he left in 1942 or 1943to work at the shipyards on the Mississippi gulf coast. Jesse worked as a carpenter and a farmer. Jesse worked hard and played hard, but was demanding and seems to have been very self centered and selfish. He made Minnie Mae account for all the food put on the table, and he kept his whiskey locked up. Jesse Dee was hard on his children, especially Vernon. Vernon could not or would not do anything that made Jesse Dee happy. We have found many pictures of family gatherings of the Presley and Hood families, but we have not found one picture of Jesse Dee or Vernon at any of these gatherings. We have not found any picture of Minnie Mae and Jesse Dee together. Noah Presley and Minnie Mae Hood Presley are at the family gatherings but not Jesse Dee or Vernon. Either the family did not like Jesse Dee or he did not like them. Jesse Dee left East Tupelo about 1942 or 1943 and did not come back. He moved around and ended up in Louisville, Kentucky. He may have received a divorce from Minnie Mae in 1945 in Kentucky. Normally the divorce would have been granted in the County where the couple had lived. Jesse was sometimes called J. D. Presley. This has been a source of confusion for past researchers because Jesse Dee had a cousin named John Delton Presley. John Delton's 1954 divorce record in the Lee County,

Mississippi Chancery Clerks office, recorded in the name of Mr. and Mrs. J. D. Presley is often mistaken as the divorce record of Jesse Dee and Minnie Mae Hood Presley. In 1954, Jesse Dee was already married to his second wife in Kentucky and had been married to her since December 1948.

Jesse Dee Presley married Vera K. Leftwich on December 4, 1948 in Louisville, Jefferson County, Kentucky. This was the second marriage for both of them. Jesse stated that his occupation was woodworker. On the marriage application, Jesse Dee states that his father's name is John Presley and his mother's name is Rosie Wesson. Jesse Dee lied on the application because he did not want his new wife to know that he was the illegitimate son of John Wallace. This lie has led to numerous errors made by researchers trying to track the roots of Elvis Presley. There never was a John Presley in Itawamba County, and Rosella was never married. Jesse Dee's mother was a Presley, not a Wesson. Jesse Dee's great grandmother was Millie Bowen Wesson. Jesse Dee's father was John Wallace. Jesse Dee told the truth about his father's first name, but not the last name. Jesse did the same with his mother's name. We believe that all of Rosella's children knew who their fathers were. They were living in a small house in a small community, how could they not know who was visiting their mother.

After Jesse Dee left East Tupelo and moved to Kentucky, he worked as a night watchman at the Pepsi Cola Plant in Louisville, Kentucky. After Elvis became famous, Jesse Dee recorded a 45 record with songs "Swinging in the Orchard",

The Roots of Elvis

"Stop Kicking My Dog Around", and "The Billy Goat Song". We believe these to be songs that Jesse Dee would have learned from his fiddle-playing father, John Wallace.

Jesse Dee McDowell Presley died March 19, 1973 of heart disease at the Methodist Hospital in Louisville, Kentucky. Vernon did attend the funeral, but we do not believe the father and son ever reconciled their differences. We have a picture of the flower arrangement that Elvis sent to Jesse Dee's funeral.

Jessse Dee McDowell Presley

Courtesy Of Patsy Presley Pressnall

Old Baptist Church At Richmond Attended By Mary Jane Presley Family Members

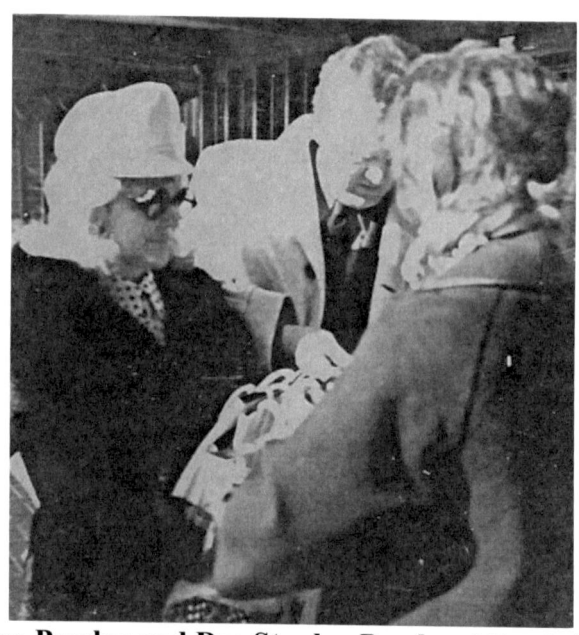

**Vernon Presley and Dee Stanley Presley Attended The Funeral Of Jesse Dee Presley   March 1973
Courtesy Of Patsy Presley Pressnall**

The Roots of Elvis

Log Cabin Built In Itawamba County Built By Joshua Hood, Great Great Grandfather Of Elvis Presley Courtesy Of Jesse And Patricia Worthey

A Mess of Blues

Vernon Elvis Presley, second son of Jesse Dee and Minnie Mae Hood Presley, was born north of Fulton, Itawamba County, Mississippi, on April 10, 1916. The location is 34 degrees 20.823'North 88 degrees 20.828'west. Mackey Hargett purchased this site in early 2009. The State of Mississippi erected a Historical Marker on the site in June 2009. Had we not started the research for this book, the location of this site would still be unknown except for a few people in Itawamba County. Mackey welcomes any interested fans to come to Itawamba County and visit the birthplace of Vernon Elvis Presley.

We know very little of Vernon's early life in Itawamba County. His father was a hard demanding person, and Vernon was not an ambitious man. He was a good looking, easy going young man that had a hard time staying at any job for very long. He tried, but always had a hard time providing for his family. Much of his early life he lived with the help of friends, relatives, and neighbors. Vernon was about eight years old when Jesse Dee moved his family to East Tupelo. We do not know when or where Vernon would have started to school, but East Tupelo Consolidated School was completed in 1926 and was located very close to the J. D. Presley home. Vernon could have attended this school for a short time. He had an opportunity to receive an education, if he had wanted to. Vernon's uncle Noah P. Presley drove a school bus for the East Tupelo Consolidated School. At that time, many school bus drivers got their jobs because of political connections. The drivers owned the buses and were paid to transport the children. We believe that Noah's father was a wealthy man with many political connections. During the depression and WWWII, cars were in short supply and during the war people had to have ration books to purchase gas or tires; Noah used his school bus to transport family and friend to many of the places they needed to go.

When Vernon was sixteen, he met a young woman that has just moved with her mother and family to East Tupelo. Twenty year old Gladys Smith had moved from east of Saltillo, Lee County, Mississippi to a house on Berry Street in East Tupelo. The Smith family had lived through hard times all of Gladys' life. The family was always moving from one farm to another to help the owner of the farm make his crop of cotton or corn. Gladys' father, Robert Lee "Bob" Smith, had died about 1931 and the family had no one to help support them. Like many of the local farm girls, Gladys gave up farm work and started working at the Tupelo Garment Company, at 495 South Green Street, Tupelo, Mississippi. Over 80% of the work force for Tupelo Garment Company lived outside of Tupelo. Every day buses were sent out to bring the farm girls into Tupelo and take them home every afternoon. This is how Gladys started working at the garment factory in Tupelo. My uncle Alwyn Westmoreland drove one of the busses used to transport the girls to Tupelo and back. Alwyn worked for Doty Brothers Motor Company at 400 South Spring Street. This was next door to Reed Manufacturing and two blocks from Tupelo Garment Company. Alwyn lived at Richmond, so all he had to do was stop and pick up the girls on his way to work. Although the wages at the garment factories were low, this employment provided cash money for families that had no other source of cash during the depression. My mother Jewell Erin Westmoreland and Aunt Mittie Westmoreland Hussey quit school and worked for Reed Manufacturing. They sometimes rode Uncle Alwyn's bus to work and with their earnings were able to help my grandfather save his farm from foreclosure.

Courtesy Of Oren Dunn Museum   Tupelo, Mississippi

Gladys Smith became close friends with Mrs. Faye Harris because they worked near each other at the Tupelo Garment Company. Faye Harris lived on Adams Street in East Tupelo. When the Smith family moved into town, they could have moved to South Tupelo or to East Tupelo. We believe that when the Smith family moved to a house on a corner lot on Berry and Adams Street, across Berry Street from the Assembly of God Church would be constructed, it was because Gladys' friend Faye Harris lived on Adams Street, across the street from Smiths. Gladys also had two uncles, Sims E. Mansell and Gains Mansell living in the East Tupelo area. They were the first preachers at the Assembly of God Church where the Presley families would later attend. The small wooden church that Elvis attended would be constructed about 1938. Having relatives and friends living in East Tupelo would have been very important to Gladys. The Jesse Dee Presley family lived on the Old Saltillo Road, about two blocks from the Smith family. To the Smiths, the Presley family looked to be well to do. Jesse Dee worked, they owned their home, and Noah Presley owned a grocery store.

Houses in the Mill Town Area of South Tupelo

Bob & Doll Mansell Smith – Gladys' parents on their wedding day. Courtesy of Corinne Richards Tate

Octavia Luvenia Mansell "Doll" Smith

At twenty years old, Gladys was starting to look like she might be an old maid. Some girls were getting married as young as fourteen. At first, Gladys dated Vernon's brother, Vester, but Gladys did not like him. To Gladys, sixteen-year-old Vernon would have looked like a very good catch. The two were attracted to each other and spent much time together. In an interview with Jerry Hopkins, Faye Harris said, "I remember seeing Mr. Presley. He was going with other girls at the time. Then he and Gladys got to going together, going to the roller rink in town or having picnics over at the fish hatchery. The hatchery was one of the nicest places we had in those days, with trees to sit under and a nice lake to look at. They did not go together too long until they got married. They went down in Verona about five miles from here. They just run off and did it one day. They sure was a handsome couple; him so blond and her so dark; and both of them happy as kids on the day that school lets out." The skating rink was located at 409 East Main Street and was operated by Theo K. (Red) Conway. They also would go to the Tupelo Fish Hatchery in South Tupelo, for picnics and fishing. The Fish Hatchery was a favorite meeting place for young people in the 30's and 40's. Without much planning or thought, the two could wait no longer. On June 17, 1933, Vernon Presley and Gladys Smith, with the help of Marshall Brown and Vona Mae Presley Brown, started out on an adventure that was to have a huge impact on music all over the world. Vona Mae Presley was Noah Presley's oldest daughter and was Vernon's first cousin. Marshall Brown was a distant cousin and schoolmate of Gladys Smith. Marshall Brown and Vona Mae had been married October 1, 1931 in Verona, Lee County, Mississippi by Justice of the Peace, Robert Emmit Kelly. They knew how to get Vernon and Gladys married. Vernon had two problems. Number one was the fact that he had just turned seventeen years old; Jesse Dee did not like Gladys and was never going to give his permission for the two to marry. Second, he did not have the money to buy the marriage license or pay the Justice of the Peace. Marshall Brown solved both problems for the two lovebirds. Marshall drove them to the Circuit Clerks Office in Pontotoc, Mississippi to get the license; they lied about their ages, Vernon claiming to be 21 and Gladys claiming to be 18. Marshall Brown paid for the marriage license, then took them to Verona, in Lee County and paid Robert Emmit Kelly to marry them. Verona is about four miles south of East Tupelo. In a 1956 interview Vernon was asked where they were married; Vernon said "We didn't elope very far; we just went down the road to Verona and got married."

Thus, the parents of Elvis Presley were wed, but they did not live happily ever after. Vernon and Gladys did not have a place to live; Vernon did not have a job or any prospects of one. The newlyweds stayed with different family members in East Tupelo, first the Smiths and then the Presleys. Gladys continued to work at the Tupelo Garment Company. Vernon worked odd jobs for Orville Bean and sometimes the Keith brothers at their garage on East Main Street in East Tupelo.

Gladys did not conceive until about nine months after the marriage. Several months after she became pregnant she had to quit work at the garment factory. She was reported to have had a hard pregnancy. Vernon borrowed money from Mr. Orville Bean to build his family a small two-room house on a lot next door to Jesse Dee Presley. These small houses were called shotgun houses because you could fire a shotgun through the front door all the way through the house and out the back door and not hit anything. Jesse Dee and Vernon's brother, Vester, helped Vernon build the house. This is believed to be where Elvis Presley was born, on January 8, 1935.

Vernon Presley And Gladys Presley On Their Wedding Day

**Gaines And Sims E. Mansell
Courtesy Of Corinne Richards Tate**

The Roots of Elvis

Christmas Program At The Church   Early 1950's
Courtesy Of Sybil Presley

Moving The Assembly Of God Church   About 1958
Courtesy of David Duncan

**Dinner On The Ground   Early 1950's
Courtesy Of Sybil Presley**

Church Being Used As A House

The Roots of Elvis

**Elvis Presley's Birthplace.
Photos taken by Mackey Hargett in 1959.**

The Roots of Elvis

Much has been written about the birth of Elvis Presley. Many people have memories of having been there when Elvis was born, and of the time that he was born. Gladys's labor lasted for about twelve hours. In that time, every woman in East Tupelo could have come by to check on Gladys. They were all telling the truth about being there when Elvis Presley was born. There can only be one truth as to the circumstances of the birth. Dr. William Robert Hunt was the physician who attended the birth of the twin boys. Dr. Hunt was the doctor used by the Tupelo Garment Company to take care of their employees. For every year of his practice, he kept a record of every birth he attended. His records indicate that on the night of January 7-8, 1935, Dr. Hunt attended Gladys Presley at home on the old Saltillo Road in East Tupelo. He noted in his baby book that at 4:00 A. M. a stillborn baby was delivered. At 4:35, a second baby boy was delivered. Elvis Aaron Presley was the surviving son. Jessie Garon Presley was buried by Pegues Funeral Home in an unmarked grave at Priceville Cemetery, Lee County, Mississippi. After the funeral of Jesse Garon, Gladys and Elvis were taken to the Tupelo Hospital on Main Street and remained there for about two weeks.

The location of the grave of Jesse Garon has been a topic of speculation by many Elvis fans. We can understand why the grave was not marked at that time because the family was very poor, but why did the family not place a marker after they could afford to? Gladys would have known where the child was buried, but cemeteries will change the way they look over a period of time. More tombstones are added, bushes and trees are cut down, other bushes and trees are planted. Losing an unmarked burial is a real possibility. After Gladys had died, we do not believe that Elvis or Vernon could find the grave. We have interviewed one family member who believes he remembers the location of the burial. Freddy Brown is the son of Marshall Brown and Vona Mae Presley Brown. His parents are the couple that drove Gladys and Vernon to Pontotoc and then to Verona to be married. Freddy is related to Elvis on both the Smith side and on the Presley side of his family. Very few people are related to Elvis on both sides of his family. Freddy remembers visiting the burial site when attending funerals of other family members. Marshall and Vona Mae were living in East Tupelo when Jesse Garon was buried; they would have known where he was buried.

Tupelo Hospital Where Gladys And Elvis Stayed After The Birth Of Elvis, The Car In Front May Be The Car That Belonged To Doctor Hunt

Freddy Brown And Rachel Ann Harden At Priceville Cemetery East Of Tupelo, Mississippi   Freddy Remembers Visiting The Grave Of Jesse Garon Presley

Freddy Brown told us another story that he remembered about Elvis. In 1957 Marshall, Vona Mae and Freddy visited the Presley family at their home on Audubon Drive in Memphis. While the families visited inside the house, Elvis and Freddy went outside to the swimming pool. Elvis showed Freddy an alligator swimming in the pool, saying, "This is my body guard." Marshall came out of the house and warned Freddy to not get too close to the pool. Elvis then got into the pool with the four-foot alligator and swam around with it. This made quite an impression on the young eight-year-old boy.

Jailhouse Rock

About 8:30 on Sunday night, April 5, 1936 the fourth deadliest tornado in United States history moved in a northeast direction through Lee County, Mississippi. Over 200 people were killed. Gladys and one-year-old Elvis were witness to this tornado. Their little house was not damaged but property across the road was. This may have caused some of Gladys lifelong worry about protecting Elvis.

Gladys was to suffer another of her heartbreaks on April 13, 1937 when her mother, Octavia Luvenia "Doll" Mansell Smith, died. Doll had been sickly much of her married life, but she gave birth to nine children and out lived her husband Robert Lee "Bob" Smith by five years. Doll was living with one of her daughters when she died. Pegues Funeral Home buried Doll beside her husband in an unmarked grave at Springhill Cemetery east of Saltillo, Lee County, Mississippi. The county paid the $15.00 cost of the funeral. Gladys has now lost her father, her mother, and her first-born son. She is alone except for relatives, girl friends, and Elvis, and it is going to get worse.

A member of the Keith family told us a story about Elvis and Vernon. The Keith family operated a garage on East Main Street in East Tupelo. They would sometimes give Vernon work cleaning up around the garage. The building at that time was heated by a large iron wood or coal-burning heater that sometimes set in the middle of the building. One day Vernon had little Elvis with him as he was working, and Elvis backed into the heater and burned the back of his leg. I would guess that

Vernon was afraid to go home with Elvis crying, and tell Gladys what had happened. This might help explain why Gladys was always worried about Elvis and never wanted him out of her sight. Many of the young boys thought that Elvis was a mamma's boy, but that may have been Gladys fault; not Elvis's.

**Orville Bean at Martins Grocery Store   About 1936
Courtesy Of Billie Martin Clayton**

Vernon continued to have a hard time supporting his young family. This continuing lack of money was the cause of a disaster for this young family. In October of 1937, Vernon sold a hog to Mr. Orville Bean for four dollars. Orville was a local businessman who owned a farm south of East Tupelo, and sometimes gave Vernon and Jesse Dee work. Orville Bean had

The Roots of Elvis

loaned Vernon the money to build the little shotgun house. Vernon thought the hog was worth more than the four-dollar check he received. Vernon probably had been paid less than the true value of the hog. Vernon let Luther Gable and Travis Smith take the check and copy Orville Bean's signature on to other checks. Luther and Travis cashed the checks and gave Vernon some of the money. Orville Bean filled charges against the three men with the Lee County sheriff. The three young men were arrested and placed in the Lee County jail. On November 17, 1937, the Tupelo Journal reported that Travis Smith (brother of Gladys Smith Presley) Luther Gable and Vernon Presley were indicted for forgery and placed under bonds of $500. All three pled not guilty to the charge of forgery. There is no mention of Vernon Presley in the Circuit Court documents on this date. Forgery is the only description of the offense in the court records. On January 4, 1938, the $500.00 bonds were filed for Travis Smith and Luther Gable; but no mention of a bond filing for Vernon Presley. Jesse Dee Presley and Henry Green Brown helped make bond for Travis Smith, but they let Vernon stay in jail. Jesse Dee helped make bond for Travis Smith and let his own son stay in jail. Why would a father do that? We already know that Jesse Dee and Vernon did not like each other. We also know that a 21-year-old Vernon was having a hard time providing for his family. We also know that Vernon did not own a hog. He had no place to keep a hog, no way to feed a hog, and no way to kill and dress a hog. The hog that Vernon sold to Orville Bean did not belong to Vernon Presley. So whom did the hog belong to? We believe that his desperate condition caused Vernon to sell a hog that belonged to his father, Jesse Dee Presley. Jesse Dee did not file charges against his own son, but he did refuse to make bond to get Vernon out of jail. So Vernon sat in jail until May 25, 1938 when all three men plead guilty to forgery and were sentenced by Judge Thomas J. Johnson to three years in the state prison at Parchman. Vernon's Uncle Noah Presley offered to pay Orville Bean for his loss of money, but once Mr. Bean had filed charges, there was nothing he could do to drop the charges. The charges were a felony, and once filed they cannot be dropped by Mr. Bean. Orville Bean did later write a letter to Mississippi Governor Hugh White asking for an early release from prison for Vernon. We have found a copy of that letter.

The Presley Family Before Vernon Goes To Prison

Vernon was received at Parchman on June 1, 1938 and was assigned a number 12231. At this time, Vernon was twenty-two years old, and he must have felt very scared and alone. In the course of our research, we were privy to view a document that records Vernon's physical examination and description. The twenty two year old Vernon was described as five feet ten and one-half inches tall and weighing one hundred forty seven pounds. The document goes on to describe an oval face, concave nose, arched eyebrows, small mouth with good teeth, medium complexion, slender build, sandy hair, blue eyes and a shoe size of nine. Vernon's body was described as having nine brown moles on his chest and an irregular scar on his right inner wrist. Vernon's religious affiliation was listed as "none". The document indicates that Vernon had a fifth grade education and that he could read and write. This is the only definitive source we have seen concerning Vernon's education. The document was signed Vernon Elvis Presley.

Parchman was not a good place to be in 1930's. The prison was like a large farm, and the prisoners had to work very hard every day. The Mississippi delta can be a very hot, humid, uncomfortable place to be locked up. We do not know what life was like for Vernon while at Parchman, but punishment was harsh for those who did not produce as they were expected to. Vernon had never been a good worker, so we believe he may have punished often. For the remainder of his life Vernon was careful to not be seen without his shirt on. Mackey Hargett has provided us a picture of Vernon on a diving board at Graceland without his shirt on.

Vernon And Elvis About 1945

The Roots of Elvis

Vernon on diving board at Graceland's swimming pool. Rickey Stanley on back of board.

Photo taken by Mackey Hargett.

The Roots of Elvis

Photo of Graceland's Pool and surrounding backyard area. Mackey Hargett enjoyed swimming there with the family. Photo taken by Mackey while on a visit with the family.

Vernon Presley and Rickey Stanley in pool at Graceland. Photo taken by Mackey Hargett.

Tupelo Fish Hatchery in South Tupelo

Life became even harder for Gladys and Elvis while Vernon was locked up. They were not able to make payments on the little two-room house, so they lost it and had to move. Gladys and Elvis lived with friends and relatives in East Tupelo for a while but we do not find that Jesse Dee was being much help to his son's family. He was probably still angry about the loss of his hog. Gladys did get some help from Vernon's Uncle Noah Presley. Noah had a large family of his own but he was always available when another family member needed help.

Sales Presley, first cousin to Vernon, and Annie Cloyd Presley, friend of Gladys from the Tupelo Garment Company, are living one house south of Gladys and Elvis in 1937. They would have been good comfort and support for Gladys at this rough period of her life. Annie and Gladys would remain friends all of their lives. Gladys and Elvis lived with different family and friends in East Tupelo but they left East Tupelo in 1938 and moved in with Gladys first cousin, Frank Richards, his wife Leona, and their children on Maple Street in South Tupelo. Frank was the son of Doll's Mansell Smith's older sister, Melissa Mansell Richards. This area of South Tupelo was called Mill Town. It was an area much like East Tupelo made up of rows of small shotgun houses and duplex apartments. Many of these houses are still occupied today. This area of South Tupelo is still called Mill Town, because this is where the Tupelo Cotton Mill was built in 1901. L. D. Hines was the first President of the Cotton Mill; John Clark of Verona was the Vice President; John R. Dobbs the Secretary and Treasurer. The directors were Private John Allen, S. T. Harkey, Shelby Topp, B. M. Dillard, Lee Joiner, and C. P. Long. Mr. Joshua Heard Ledyard was elected manager of the Cotton Mill in 1905.

Because the Cotton Mill could not sell some of the cloth it produced, Tupelo Garment Company was started in 1921 as a separate department of the Cotton Mill with the installation of 24 sewing machines. This allowed the mill to turn excess cloth into clothing. In 1923 the Tupelo Garment Company was organized with Brit A. Rogers the first president; Rex F. Reed; from Tilden; as Vice-President; John P. Hunter Secretary and Treasurer. By 1925, the company was operating 60 sewing machines. In 1926, William B. Field became General Superintendent of the Tupelo Garment Company. The first separate building of the Tupelo plant was constructed in 1931. Tupelo Garment also built plants in many of the surrounding towns. This made it easier for the employees to get to work because the plants were closer to their homes. In 1933, the three-story unit of the Tupelo Plant was built. The Tupelo Garment Company was now operating 1000 sewing machines and employing 1400 people. This is when Gladys Smith and many local farm girls started working in Tupelo for the garment company. The building containing the cotton mill was later used as J. J. Rogers and Sons Wholesale for many years. The buildings housing the cotton mill and the garment company are still standing.

Mr. Joshua Heard Ledyard was the president and general manager of the Tupelo Cotton Mill. Mr. Ledyard was born on September 3, 1875 at Shubuta, Mississippi. Mr. Ledyard attended A & M College at Starkville, Mississippi, and graduated in 1892. He later studied for two years at Lowell Textile Institute in Lowell, Massachusetts. He accepted a position as assistant manager of the Meridian Cotton Mill in Meridian, Mississippi. In 1905, he was offered the position of general superintendent at the newly formed Tupelo Cotton Mill. His ideas were somewhat different from other mill owners. Mr. Ledyard built a home on South Church Street in the Mill Town area. He believed that the workers would be happier and more efficient if they had good living conditions. He had the same type of houses built in Mill Town that you would find in East Tupelo, but he made sure that were kept repaired and painted. The grounds of the mill and the yards of the houses were kept neat and clean. Each house had its own vegetable garden and a fenced yard. Mr. Ledyard provided a baseball field, basketball court, and tennis court for the use of the mill workers. He built an outdoor stage with a grandstand for social and public events. His company gave free medical treatment to the employees and their families. The company had a band that was one of the best in Northeast Mississippi. Thanks to Mr. Ledyard, Mill Town would have been a good place for the mill families to live.

    Mr. Ledyard believed in educating the children, so he had a primary school built on South Broadway Street. This was known as the Ledyard Primary School, and was built to provide an early education for the children of Mill Town. The school was in easy walking distance for the children of the mill workers. The best teachers available were hired for the school. A story in the Tupelo Daily Journal, January 17, 1930, reported the enrollment at Ledyard's School has increased so much that it has become necessary to add another teacher for full time, Mrs. Francis Beard. The auditorium has been converted into a very comfortable schoolroom for Mrs. Beard and her twenty-five little people, and the congestion in the first grade has been greatly relieved. At the end of last month, the enrollment was as follows; first grade, sixty-five; second grade, thirty-eight; third grade, thirty-five; fourth grade, thirty-three. Some of the teachers were Mrs. Carrie Mae Wright, Mrs. Douglas Hunter, Miss Nell Huey, and Mrs. Standard Topp.

Frank Richards

Gladys cousin, Frank Richards, lived across Maple Street from the Ledyard School with the cotton mill and garment factory within walking distance of his house. This area was considered the wrong side of the tracks, but it was the perfect place for Gladys and Elvis while Vernon was in prison. Two train tracks were located less than 100 yards from where Gladys and Elvis lived. Billy Stanley, stepbrother of Elvis, said Elvis told him that the train whistle at night was the most lonesome sound he had ever heard. Elvis would have been living with his mother on Maple Street in South Tupelo; his father in prison for fifteen months or off at work much of the time. From age three until seven would have been a very sad time for little Elvis. For much of that time Elvis had only his mother to hold on to. For most of Elvis's childhood, women raised him with very little influence from his father.

The GM&O Rebel Came Through Tupelo When Elvis Lived On Maple Street In South Tupelo

    The depression had hit the United States in the early 1930's. This caused hard time all over the south, and hit the cotton mills especially hard. The market for their cloth bottomed out. Cotton mill workers saw their jobs disappear or their paychecks shrink. The mill workers in South Tupelo saw their lives changing. In 1938 outside unions showed up to organize the mill workers and demand more money for the employees. The union called for a sit down strike for better wages, which the mill could not pay. The result was that the mill shut down, and life in Mill Town would never be the same. This closing of the mill broke Mr. Ledyard's heart. This was the Mill Town that Gladys and Elvis moved into while Vernon was in Parchman prison.

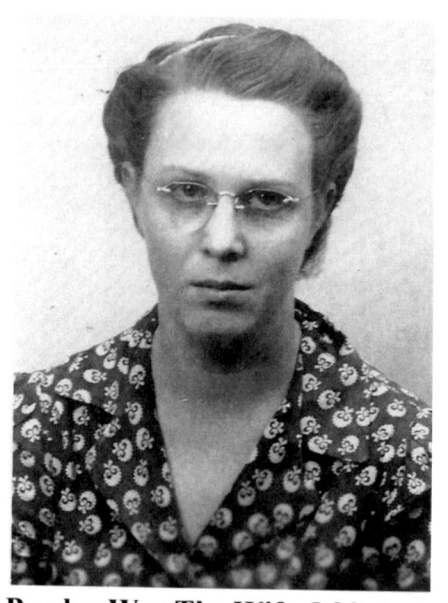

Annie Cloyd Presley Was The Wife Of Sales Presley And Best Friend To Gladys Presley   Annie And Sales Attended The Same Church In East Tupelo As The Presleys Courtesy Of Sybil Presley

My Aunt Zora Riley was one of Gladys' friends in East Tupelo. Aunt Zora had talked to us about going with Gladys and Elvis on a bus to visit Vernon at Parchman. I had always pictured all of the girl friends going down to the bus station on Troy Street and waiting for the Greyhound bus to take them on the long trip to

Parchman Prison. That was not the way the bus trips happened. Noah Presley again came to their rescue. Noah Presley had a school bus because he had a contract with the Lee County school system to carry children to and from the East Tupelo Consolidated School. Noah also used this bus to carry his large family just about everywhere they went. When Gladys needed to visit Vernon at Parchman, Noah would use his school bus to take Gladys, Elvis and any of their friends that could make the visit on that long trip to Parchman. At four years of age, Elvis would have been riding on a school bus with a group of young adults on an adventure to visit his father in prison. Now I can better understand what Aunt Zora was talking about.

Noah Presley's School Bus   Courtesy Of Freddy Brown

Vernon was released from Parchman on February 6, 1939. Orville Bean and other local people had written letters to the governor of Mississippi asking him to give Vernon an early release from prison. Vernon was not yet 23 years old. When he returned home his family continued to live in South Tupelo not East Tupelo. In May of 1939, Vernon started to work for the Lee County Sanitation Department. Vernon worked for Lee County until November of 1940. Vernon held this job for eighteen months. That was one of the longest periods Vernon ever stayed at one job. Vernon and Gladys continued to live at several locations on Maple Street in South Tupelo because Gladys had relatives there and the location was convenient for Gladys to work at the garment factory. Getting to downtown Tupelo was also much easier from Maple Street. Several small grocery stores were located in Mill Town. Just north of the railroad tracks was the Tupelo Cotton Oil Company. This business processed cottonseed for the oil, and it made all of the south part of Tupelo smell wonderful. The cottonseed was a byproduct of the ginning of locally grown cotton. The Tupelo Cotton Oil Mill was founded in 1899 with Mr. John Clark from Verona as the president, James Henderson Strain as vice-president, and Clark Raymond Strain as the treasurer.

    The icehouse was also located just north of the railroad tracks. Ice was important because no one had refrigerators. A block of ice was delivered to each house in Tupelo by truck or by horse and wagon every day. You could hang a sign on your back door indicating the amount of ice you needed, and the iceman would bring the ice into your house and put it into the icebox. Too bad those days are gone. The icehouse would also crush ice for individuals so that they could make homemade ice cream. The making of homemade ice cream was a fun time for the kids back then.

Elvis Presley With His Wagon At The Farrar Home In East Tupelo About 1942

The Roots of Elvis

Presley Family About 1942

The Small White House In The Upper Right Side Of The Picture May Be The House Elvis And Gladys Lived In Oren Dunn Museum   Tupelo, Mississippi

Grocery Store And Service Station In South Tupelo The Presley Family would Have Shopped Here

The Roots of Elvis

Vernon Elvis Presley

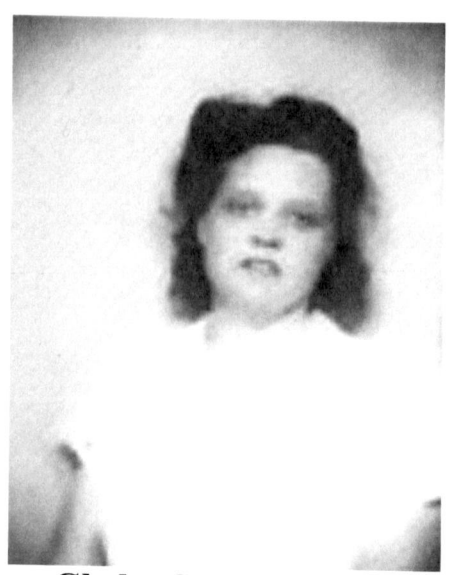

Gladys Smith Presley

That's Alright Mama

In November of 1940, Vernon and Gladys are living at 510 ½ Maple Street in South Tupelo. We also believe that Vernon would not return to East Tupelo as long as Jesse Dee was living there. We do not know all the jobs Vernon would have had in 1941. Vernon worked for Leake and Goodlett Lumber Yard for a part of 1941. Leake and Goodlett sold building materials and were also in the home building business. Vernon would have worked in construction as a carpenter and sometimes painter. Vernon could have easily walked to work from his home in South Tupelo. Vernon found work wherever he could, but some of his jobs required him to be out of town much of the time.

In September of 1941, Elvis starts to school in the first grade, but not at East Tupelo Consolidated school in East Tupelo. Elvis would have started to school at the Ledyard Primary School in South Tupelo. I was having a hard time trying to reconcile Elvis living in South Tupelo and going to the first grade in East Tupelo. All of the friends and family talked about Gladys walking Elvis to school each day. They also talked about Elvis sitting on the front porch watching for his mother to come home from work. Elvis going to school at the Ledyard School would explain both of these stories. The Ledyard School was one-half blocks from where Gladys and Vernon lived. This would have been an easy walk for Gladys and Elvis. The Tupelo Garment Factory was located at 495 South Green Street. This was about two blocks from where the Presley family lived. Elvis could have sat on the porch and watched his mother leave work and walk down Maple Street coming home to him each day.

Sometime in 1941, Vernon goes to work for S & W Construction in Sardis, Mississippi. He worked there until January of 1942. He also worked for J. A. Jones Construction Company Inc. in Ozark, Alabama for a short time. Then he worked for the Ferguson Oman Gulf Ordinance plant at Prairie, Mississippi. This large operation was making ammunition for the War effort. Some of the buildings are still in use today. Because of the war, Vernon had a choice of many jobs in the early 1940's.

During the war years, Tupelo provided a club for the soldiers called the Uniform Club. It was located in the south part of Tupelo, on the corner of Magazine Street and Spring Street, near the Union Station Depot. This was in easy walking distance for soldiers waiting for the train. My uncle Carl Riley was a member of the first paratrooper military unit the United States created. He was killed in February 1943 in North Africa. Many local men served in the military, but Vernon did not. That may have been because Vernon was a convicted felon. We do not know for sure. With Gladys and Vernon both working, the Presley family should have been prosperous at this time in their lives, but they do not appear to have been capable of improving their lives.

Memories

In our research for the roots of Elvis, I have had many people tell me stories about their relationship with or stories they know about Elvis. We also talked to people who attended school with Elvis and people who lived next door to Elvis that had no memory of him. Many of the East Tupelo memories had to do with his singing the song "Old Shep" at school. Many of the Tupelo memories were about Elvis taking his guitar with him everywhere he went.

Eugene D. (Ed) Christian is a local historian and friend of mine who has a story I had never heard about Elvis Presley. Ed gave me his story and I will record it as he told me. "My first recollection of Elvis was when he and his mother moved to Maple Street in old South Tupelo sometime during World War II. I remember that Elvis was at first somewhat shy around me and my friends, but he soon blended in. Most of the time, Elvis seemed sad, but he was happy to have new friends, and to be a member of our little gang. We were not a bunch of hooligans, but we were perhaps a little mischievous, not so much as to harm anyone. My Great Aunt Perl called Jackie Stevens, James Harold Lloyd, Jerald Tackett, Jackie Clark, myself, and Elvis the "Wild Bunch". Sadly, all but I have passed away.

I remember the corncob wars we had with rival groups, not like enemies, more like friendly competitors, although at times the wars could get heated especially if someone slipped in a slingshot. In one of these wars, Elvis was hit in the back of the head leaving a good size knot; he never cared much for corncob wars after that. He always enjoyed our "chicken raids". On

The Roots of Elvis

south Green Street, just south of the Kings Creek Bridge, there was a large abandoned cattle barn, a grain silo, four or five one room shacks, and wild chickens. It was these wild chickens we would chase and sometimes catch. I remember us taking them down into Kings Creek and trying to roast them over an open fire.

I remember the time we laid in wait on top of the old livery stable on North Spring Street for Tupelo Police Officer, Mr. Ed Conn, to walk by. When he did, we would drop balloons filled with water in front of him. However, Elvis dropped his balloon late, hitting Officer Conn. We got down quickly from that building and ran. At that time, Officer Conn was in his 60's, and there was no way he could catch us.

I remember the time Elvis and I borrowed Fred Ingellis's guitar. We wanted to serenade a couple of very cute sisters, and they invited us in. Elvis leaned the guitar against a post on the front porch and forgot that it was there, until a clap of thunder reminded us. Apparently, it had been raining for some time because the guitar was filled with water and was ruined. Elvis promised Mr. Ingellis he would pay for the guitar, but he never did.

I remember that my Aunt Floy Mae Frost and Gladys were good friends and both moved to Memphis about the same time. My Uncle Buster Frost and Aunt Floy moved to Memphis where Buster had a job keeping up a tract of rental houses just off South Cooper Parkway. Aunt Floy contacted Gladys and they began visiting. After Elvis moved into Graceland, he would send a car over to my Aunt Floy's house to bring her to

Graceland for lunch and sometimes for dinner. These visits continued until Mrs. Gladys death.

I lost touch with Elvis after they moved to Memphis, until I ran into him on a street in Frankfort, Germany in the late 50's. I had enlisted in the Mississippi National Guard and after about three months, I transferred to the regular army. We were both in the Third Army, Third Armored Division but in different companies. Even then he had his hanger-on's. We stood on the street and talked about old times for a short while, but Colonel Parker seemed nervous about our talking of old times, and he wanted to go.

Early in his music career, Elvis was generous to a fault, giving away new cars and money, almost as if he was trying to buy friends. With all his fame and money, Elvis was just a poor unhappy boy from East Tupelo, trapped in a world he could not control. Many people have claimed to have known Elvis, and many fabrications have been concocted of him and places he is supposed to be connected with.

The next time Elvis and I met was in the mid 60's here in Tupelo. On that day, Richard Hill and I were returning to work at Western Auto after eating lunch. Richard's family operated the Western Auto store. We were walking south on North Spring Street and as we came to Phillips Seed and Hardware store I noticed a long black limousine parked in front of Phillips. I remember saying to Richard "I wonder who belongs to that" We had taken only a few steps, when we heard someone calling my name. We turned to see who it was, and it was Elvis, half in and half out of that black limousine. I told Richard that I would be on in a few minutes. Elvis asked me to get in, which I did. We talked about old times, and how happy we were to see each other again.

I asked Elvis what he was doing in Tupelo. He told me that his attorneys were here to reclaim an iron fence that once had been at Graceland. He had given the fence to go around a little park that was to be built for the children of East Tupelo. It seemed that the fence went elsewhere and Elvis was upset about it. We traded small talk for the next few minutes; he told me how unhappy he was and how empty his life had become. I ask how could that be, you have anything and everything you want, you're on top of the world. Elvis said" No the world is on top of me, I'm just a puppet on a string." Then Elvis said, "Gene I wish I could get out of this damned car and just walk around Tupelo without being mobbed." I can't imagine what it would be like not being able to go shopping, or to a restaurant for coffee, or just walk around without being mobbed by fans, such was his life. He then asks if I would come to work for him. He said, "It won't be physical work, just be a companion." I said no, my life is here, I'm married to a good woman and I would not wish to leave her. I guess I was the only one to say no to Elvis at this period of his life. He seemed disappointed, but then his expression could have been one of relief. This was the last time I ever saw or talked to Elvis. I have often wondered if I had said yes to his job offer, if things would have turned out differently. I also wondered if Gladys had brought Elvis that rifle instead of a guitar, how his life would have turned out.

I have never tried to capitalize from my friendship with

Elvis; just being his friend was good enough. Some things I know about Elvis are best left out of history. One thing about Elvis, he was never the macho man he often portrayed in his movie roles; however, he was not particularly wimpy either. For the remainder of my days, I shall remember Elvis and those carefree days when we ran wild in the streets of old South Tupelo. What I have stated here is true, and the truth is all that matters to me."

This may be the only time Ed Christian has been interviewed about his friendship with Elvis Presley. I asked Ed why he thought the Presley family left Tupelo. Ed said that the State of Tennessee welfare was more than the Mississippi welfare, which would be more free help, not necessarily more opportunity for work.

In a March 24, 1956 radio interview with Robert Carlton Brown, Elvis said that the only kind of trouble I have ever been in is stealing eggs when I was real little. We think the stealing eggs and the catching chickens with Ed Christian in South Tupelo both happened about the same time.

We interviewed Richard Hill about meeting Elvis, and he told us much the same story. Richard said that Gene and I had been to eat at Leon Blackwell's Café on North Spring Street across the street from the Lee County Courthouse. On our way back to work, we passed a black Cadillac parked on the street, we heard someone call out "Gene". It was Elvis. Gene asked if I wanted to meet Elvis. We walked over to the car. Elvis had sent his driver into Leon's Café to get some hamburgers. Elvis invited us into the car. Gene got in but I had to get back to work at the store so I talked to Elvis through the open window for about two minutes. I could tell that they wanted to talk about old friends and times so I shook his hand and returned to the Western Auto store at 114 North Spring Street. Gene returned to work in about fifteen minutes.

In September of 1942, Elvis started the second grade at Ledyard School in South Tupelo. Gladys would have continued the practice of walking Elvis to school each day. The last part of 1942 Vernon was working for S&W Construction Company helping build POW camps at Como, Mississippi. He then worked for Dunn Construction Company in Millington Tennessee. This employment puts Vernon in the Memphis area for some time. He lived in the company barracks and returned home to South Tupelo on the weekends. His last paycheck from Dunn Construction was February 14, 1943. Vernon then came back to Tupelo and went to work for the Pepsi Cola Bottling Company in Tupelo. Pepsi Cola was located at 316 South Broadway, Tupelo. This was three blocks from where the Presley's lived on Maple Street. We believe that Vernon continued to live at various locations in South Tupelo until he takes his family to Moss Point, Mississippi in May 1943, to work at the shipyard. Vernon waited until Elvis finished the second grade in May of 1943, and then he took his family and left for Moss Point. By giving up his house in Mill Town, and taking his family with him, we believe Vernon was planning to stay in Moss Point. He had very little reason to come back to Tupelo. If he had stayed in Moss Point, we would not have the Elvis Presley that we know today.

We have wondered why Vernon did not serve in World War II. The United States did not draft married men with children until the early part of 1943. Vernon's serving time in prison may have kept him out of the military. While living in South Tupelo, Gladys would have continued to have contact with her East Tupelo friends because she was working with them. The family would have visited and gone to church in East Tupelo. Vernon would have continued to visit his mother and siblings, but not his father, Jesse Dee. Vernon did not return to live in East Tupelo until his father had left the Tupelo area.

In May of 1943, Vernon's first cousin, Sales Presley and his wife Annie Presley went to Moss Point, along with Vernon and Gladys, to work at the shipyard. Many people from the Tupelo area went to the gulf coast to work building ships. Jobs were plentiful and the pay was good. My father tried it for a few weeks, but he got homesick and came home. Vernon had worked out of town for over a year, coming back to Tupelo on most weekends. This time Sales and Vernon took their families with them, which indicates they were planning to stay for a long time. The families lived in small one-room cabins. The heat and humidity was awful, and they did not like the smell of the coast. Elvis and Gladys did not like the seafood, and Elvis would never eat fish after this. The Mississippi Gulf Coast did not compare well to the pleasant living conditions in Mill Town. Annie Presley was pregnant and wanted to come home to Tupelo for the birth of her fourth child, Sybil who was born in December of 1943. The two young couples only stayed about five weeks on the coast before they all got homesick and returned home. When they returned to Tupelo, Jesse Dee Presley had left Tupelo

The Roots of Elvis

to work at the shipyard, so for the first time since November of 1937, Vernon returns to live in East Tupelo. Vernon was 27 when he moved his family back to East Tupelo. Vernon and Gladys had been married for ten years,

Vernon may have moved in with his mother on Old Saltillo Road until she loses her house because Jesse Dee does not send her any money. Jesse Dee never returned to Tupelo after leaving to work at the shipyard. Jesse's children were all grown, he and Minnie Mae did not like each other, and he had no reason to come back to Tupelo. Jesse did better than some men in a bad marriage; he at least stayed home until all his children were grown. We know that Vernon was back living in East Tupelo by July of 1943, and in September of 1943, Elvis starts to school in the third grade at Lawhon School. Mrs. Harvey was Elvis's third grade teacher. Elois Bedford Sandifur was Elvis's girlfriend in grade school at Lawhon. She remembered Mrs. Dillard being their fourth grade school teacher.

Mrs. Geraldine Franks Sheffield is a friend of mine who taught at Lawhon School when Elvis was a student there. She was born May 13, 1923 at Guntown, Lee County, Mississippi. Her father was William Tracy Franks and her mother was Luna Duvall Franks. Tracy Franks was born in the Unity Community of Lee County. This is the same area that the Smith family lived, and we think Tracy may have known of the Smith family before Elvis starts to school at Lawhon. Mr. Franks had taught at the Auburn School and was the assistant principal and teacher at Lawhon when Elvis was in school there. After teaching school, Mr. Franks was the elected City Clerk of Tupelo for twenty years. His family lived at 811 Allen Street, next door to James Ausborn, brother of Mississippi Slim and friend of Elvis. Geraldine told me a story of her father befriending Elvis while he was at Lawhon. He would take the family food and would give Elvis money. Mr. Franks announced to the school the talent contest to be held at the Mississippi Alabama Fair and Dairy Show in September of 1945. He encouraged Elvis to enter the contest, and may have taken him to the fair that day. Elvis actually came in fifth place in the talent contest. The winner was determined by the amount of applause from the audience. Little Elvis probably did not have many friend or family in the audience that day. Geraldine said that her father would take Elvis different places, and would sometimes give him money. She said that her father gave Gladys the money to buy the guitar for Elvis's birthday in January of 1946. She described Elvis as a sweet little boy. Geraldine said that when Elvis would come back to Tupelo, after becoming a star, he would call Tracy and take him out to lunch.

Mr. Tracy Franks

Vernon works for Dunn Construction in Millington, Tennessee for one week in June of 1943. Vernon then goes to work at L. P. McCarty and Sons in July of 1943. His job was to load the truck after the orders were pulled, and then deliver the groceries to different locations over Northeast Mississippi. Vernon seems to have stayed at L. P. McCarty and Sons until his family left Tupelo for Memphis in 1948. Five years at the same job would have been a record for Vernon. Vernon's nickname while he worked at L. P. McCarty was "jelly bean". Vernon would have walked or hitchhiked the one mile across the levy from East Tupelo to Tupelo and back to work each day. Few people were fortunate enough to own a car during the World War II. Tires and gasoline were also in very short supply. The City of Tupelo would have several organized scrap collection projects at this time to help with the war effort.

Once again, the Vernon Presley family seems to be on the road to prosperity. Vernon moved his family to 904 Kelly Street in East Tupelo. They were living next door to the Clark family, and across the street from Noah Presley's family. Noah lived at 915 Kelly Street. Marshall Brown is living across the street and Faye Harris is less than a block away on Adams Street. Gladys is living close to all of her good friends. This would have been a happy time for Gladys. On August 18, 1945, Vernon purchased a house on Berry Street in East Tupelo from Mr. Orville Bean. This was a new house, and we believe Minnie Mae is living with Vernon's family at this time. Orville Bean was the same man that purchased the hog from Vernon back in 1937. Orville had helped Vernon to get released from prison in 1939. The two men seem to have forgiven each other. Orville Bean's daughter,

Mrs. Oleta Grimes, was Elvis's fifth grade teacher at Lawhon, and she was a great help to Elvis and the Presley family. She encouraged Elvis to continue with his musical interest, and she gave the family food when they were without. Orville Bean and his daughter were better to Vernon's family than Jesse Dee Presley was.

One of Gladys friends that lived on Adams Street in East Tupelo for a while was Bernice Jenkins. Bernice was another young woman that worked at Tupelo Garment Factory. She had four children; three sons and one daughter. Her oldest son Lamar Croft was about the same age as Elvis. One Saturday Gladys and Bernice took Elvis and Lamar with them into downtown Tupelo shopping. The two boys were left to themselves to run around town while Gladys and Bernice took care of their shopping. Later in the afternoon when it was time to go home, the two mothers could not find the boys. Gladys was about to panic because she could not find Elvis. After looking for the boys for a while, they found them at Lyles Feed Store. Burton "Bert" Lyle owned the feed store that was located between Tupelo Hardware and the G M & O railroad tracks north of Main Street. Bert had moved from Tremont, Itawamba County to Tupelo about 1924. Elvis and Lamar, had climbed on top of some railroad boxcars, and they were running and jumping from one boxcar to another. This would have been very dangerous. After finding Elvis, Gladys was so happy that all she could do was hug and kiss on him. On the other hand, Lamar got a good whipping from his mother. Gladys just could not bring herself to punish little Elvis. This could be one reason some of the kids thought Elvis was a mama's boy.

The Roots of Elvis

For unknown reasons, Vernon and Gladys lost the house on Berry Street on July 18, 1946, and Vernon moved his family from East Tupelo in July of 1946. Vernon deeded the house to his friend, Aaron Kennedy, and then he moved to two different locations near L. P. McCarty and Sons wholesale grocery. At first, they lived on the corner of Commerce and East Main streets. This location is on the edge of what was known as Shake Rag in Tupelo. Shake Rag was a large area of very poor black families east of the G M & O railroad and north of East Main Street. This is the same area where my grandfather owned his livestock barn. This is an area where I rode horses as a child. It was not an area that Gladys would have allowed an eleven-year-old Elvis to spend time without her supervision. Elvis did have some black influence on his music, but it did not come from time spent in Shake Rag. In my interview with Ed Christian, I asked about any time the boys spent in the Shake Rag area. Ed said they did not go into Shake Rag but that there was a feed store on the south side of East Main Street east of the fairground where an elderly black man would sit in front of the store and play the guitar for tips. Elvis and his friends would sit and listen to this black man play the guitar. This would have been the Whisenant Feed Store.

Shake Rag In Tupelo

The Roots of Elvis

In the 1930's and 40's Tupelo had a hotel for blacks called the Panama Hotel. The hotel had a café and a barbershop, which were gathering places for local blacks. The hotel faced west at 400 South Front Street, behind the City County Building on the East side of the railroad tracks. Behind the hotel and down the hill were the fairgrounds. Any blacks getting off the train at Union Station could get a room at the Panama. Along with the Panama Hotel, there was a row of houses occupied by black families. When the Presley family lived at Mulberry Alley, the Panama Hotel was about two city blocks from their house. When the Presleys lived in South Tupelo, the Panama Hotel was about three blocks from their house. Elvis could have easily had contact with black musicians staying at the Panama Hotel.

Panama Hotel Is On The Left, Southern Hotel On The Right

**Aerial View of Downtown Tupelo
The Small House At The Bottom And Middle Of The Picture
Is The House The Presleys Lived In On Mulberry Alley**

The next place the Presley family lived was on Mulberry Alley, a street that ran east and west behind Cockrell Banana Company, and L. P. McCarty and Sons. Mulberry Alley was east of the G M & O railroad and dead ended at the railroad. South of Mulberry Alley was the fairgrounds where Elvis would make his homecoming appearance in 1956 and 1957. Mr. Earnest Bowen, who would later work as station manager for

WELO radio station, remembered the Presleys living on Mulberry Alley because his father had a cabinet shop at 119 Mulberry Alley. Earnest said that his family would take food to the Presleys who were always in need of help. This location is now in front of the Tupelo City Hall.

Charlie Boren was an early entertainment entrepreneur and D J at WELO radio station in Tupelo. Charlie was a promoter of many concerts in Tupelo in the late 1940's and early 1950's. Charlie also owned some movie theaters in the Tupelo area, and owned the sound equipment used by Elvis at the 1956 and 1957 appearances at the fair in Tupelo.

**Charlie Boren On The Air At WELO In Tupelo
Courtesy Of Billy Boren**

Charlie Boren Back Stage with Elvis At The 1956 Fair In Tupelo   Charlie Knew Elvis When He Was Hanging Around The WELO Radio In The Late 1940's   Elvis Had Hoped To Have His Own Radio Program On WELO

Courtesy Of Billy Boren

The Roots of Elvis

Tupelo High and Junior High School
Elvis Attended School In The Building On The Left

In September of 1946, Elvis enrolled in the sixth grade at Milam Junior High School. His teacher in the sixth grade was Mrs. Dewey Camp. This is the third school that Elvis has attended and the third time he was to make a new set of friends. On November 26, 1946, Mrs. Camp's homeroom presented a Thanksgiving program in the Tupelo High School auditorium. Jack McKinney gave me a copy of the program for that event. Jack had been one of the students on the program, and was listed next to Elvis Presley. Elvis played two parts in the program. He played the part of a judge in one of the skits, and the part of the month of October in another skit. Elvis's friend, James Ausborn, also had a part in the program. Elvis was not one of the nine students that sang the Pilgrim song, but it appears the singing group was all female. Joe Wallace from Tupelo was in this same thanksgiving play with Elvis, but he had no memory of going to school with Elvis. The only memory Jack McKinney had of Elvis was him bringing his guitar to school and singing Old Shep. Many of the people that lived near Elvis or went to school with Elvis have little or no memory of him.

When we started this research, I had the idea that Elvis had spent most of his life in East Tupelo. That did not prove to be correct. His first three years he lived in East Tupelo, then he lived in South Tupelo for over five years. He was back living in East Tupelo in the summer of 1943. The family moved back to Tupelo in the fall of 1946. Elvis lived in Tupelo until they left for Memphis in November of 1948. Elvis was in easy walking distance of downtown Tupelo for much of his childhood. Elvis would have spent much more time in downtown Tupelo than I had originally believed. He would have been close to the movie theaters, drug stores, hotels, restaurants, radio stations, and places his parents worked. Elvis was more of a downtown Tupelo boy than I had believed.

Lyric Theatre where Elvis Watched Movies

Allen Street runs in an east and west direction north of

Milam School. On Allen Street west of Gloster Street is Where Mississippi Slim and his brother James Ausborn lived. James was a classmate and friend of Elvis while in school at Milam. Mississippi Slim was Elvis's hero from WELO Radio Station. Tracy Franks lived next door to the Ausborn family. My friend Bob Kinney lived next door to Tracy Franks.

Tupelo Theatre Where Elvis Watched Movies

Courtesy Of Sybil Presley

Across Allen Street from the Ausborn home was an empty field where the local boys would play baseball and softball. Elvis was one of the boys that would meet at the field after school to play ball. One day when Bob Kenney was about six years old, he was watching the older boys play ball. Someone hit a foul ball that hit Bob in the head, knocking him out. All the boys scattered because they did not know how badly he was hurt. He survived with just a knot on his head. James Ausborn later told Bob that Elvis was the one that had hit the foul ball.

Mississippi Slim And His Uncle Clinton

The Presley family would continue to go to church with friends and family at the First Assembly of God Church in East Tupelo. Brother Frank Smith was their pastor, and he is the one that taught Elvis the song Old Shep. Vernon would continue to deliver groceries for L. P. McCarty and Sons. Gladys worked for Longs Laundry. Brother Frank Smith was also working in the warehouse at L. P. McCarty. Elvis would continue to carry his guitar with him just about everywhere he went and never missed a chance to sing.

Mississippi Slim Was One Elvis's Many Singing Idols

Don Whitney And His Playboys Was Another Group Of Entertainers That Played On WELO In The Late 1940's Elvis Would Have Watched And Listened To Them

September of 1947 Elvis enrolled in the seventh grade at Milam Junior High School. After living on Mulberry Alley, the Presley family lived for a short time on old Highway 45 North near the Ruff dairy farm. Sometime before September of 1947, the Presley family moved to 1010 North Green Street, Tupelo. North Green Street was on the north side of Tupelo and was once part of U S Highway 45. North Green Street was part of the black area of Tupelo, but it was not Shake Rag. North Green was referred to as "The Hill", and was the home of the more successful and affluent black families in Tupelo. Many of the houses on Green Street had been destroyed in the 1936 tornado that did so much damage to Tupelo. Some of the houses on North Green were newer than houses in the other areas the Presley family had lived. The home on 1010 Green Street was a four-room house with an indoor bathroom. This may have been the first time the family had indoor plumbing with a bathtub. What close contact Elvis had with the black community in Tupelo would have been while living on North Green Street. 1010 North Green Street is where the family lived when they left Tupelo on November 6, 1948 for Memphis, Tennessee. On February 28, 1948, Gladys took Elvis to the Lee County library so that Elvis could get a library card. This was important to Elvis and his mother, who had no better than a sixth grade education. This library card has been reprinted many times. The story has one major flaw in it. Visitors to Tupelo are sent to visit the current Lee County library on Jefferson Street in Tupelo. Elvis never set foot inside that building. Elvis would have visited the library that was replaced by the current building, but when Elvis received his library card, the Lee County library was on the other side of town.

The Roots of Elvis

City-County Building

This Building On Jefferson Street Replaced The Library In The City-County Building

The Library was located on the third floor of the City County building at 405 South Spring Street. This was three blocks from where the Presley family lived on Maple Street in Mill Town, and very close to different places that Gladys worked.

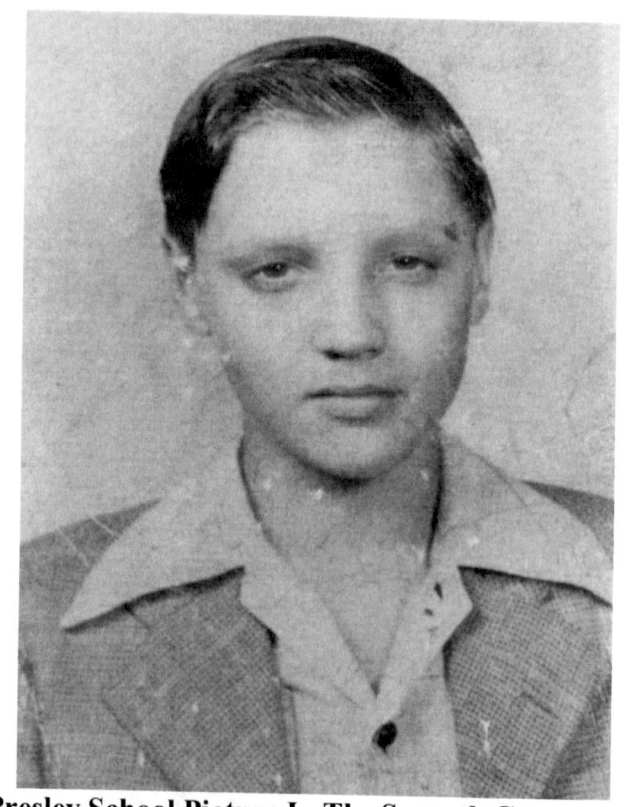

Elvis Presley School Picture In The Seventh Grade At Milam

Elvis had a new group of friends after he moved to North Green and was going to school at Milam. Friends from school were James Ausborn, Bobby Dozier, Bitsy Savery, Roland

**East Tupelo Assembly Of God Church On A Sunday In 1941
We Believe Gladys, Vernon, And Elvis Are in The Picture**

Tindall, and Billy Welch. Elvis also had friends from the black community that lived near him on Green Street. Two of the friends that lived near Elvis were Sam Bell and Ollie Janice Davis, now Mrs. Janice Scales. We met with Janice and Sam in March 2006 to view North Green Street, and have them show us where the Presley home was located. The house numbers have changed since 1948. 1010 Green Street today is not the 1010 Green Street where the Presley family lived. The lot where Elvis lived is now vacant, overgrown, and covered with trash. The Presleys rented the house from James R. Parsons who lived at 1245 North Green Street. His wife, Mrs. Lura Parsons, was a music teacher and could have helped Elvis learn to play the piano. The area was changed in the early 1970's because Green Street was moved with the construction of US Highway 78. Janice and her two brothers, Eugene and James, lived at 1207 North Green Street, about one block south of the Presley family. Janice was born in 1937, and Eugene was born in 1932. Janice's father, John Davis, was part owner of a grocery store, where the Presley family sometimes shopped, at 1209 Green Street. The store was torn down in the early 1950's. Ode Lockridge owned a grocery at 1312 North Green Street.

    Janice told us that her family owned a piano, one of the only families in the area that owned a piano. Elvis would visit at her home often because the family owned this piano. While all the kids were outside playing, Elvis would be inside with her brother, Eugene Davis, picking at the piano. This would have been one of the first pianos that Elvis had an opportunity to play, and is the only provable black influence on Elvis's music while he lived in Tupelo.

Sam Bell, Janice Scales, And Rachel Harden Looking At The Lot On North Green Street Where The Presleys Lived

Spring Hill Missionary Baptist Church At 605 N Green Street This Church Is Near Where The Presley Family Lived On North Green Street In 1947 And 1948

Sam Bell's family lived at 1025 North Green Street. Sam remembered Gladys as being nice and making the kids bologna and cheese sandwiches with Kool-Aid to drink. He remembered that Vernon was gone much of the time. He remembered Elvis wearing overalls and carrying his guitar. Sometimes Elvis would pretend that a broom was a guitar. Sam remembered Elvis having a bicycle and a pump BB gun. The kids also built a tree house to play in. I am sure that Sam, Janice and others from "The Hill" have many more Elvis stories to tell.

Billy Welch was a good friend from school and from living on North Green Street. We met Billy's sister Faye Welch, now Mrs. Faye Saxon, in May of 2006. Verona,

The Roots of Elvis

Mississippi has a festival in June of each year where we perform a reenactment of the wedding of Gladys and Vernon Presley. Faye was teaching drama at Shannon High School when we met her. She has helped us find young students to play the parts of Gladys and Vernon in the reenactment.

Faye's brother, William Claude "Billy" Welch Jr. was born October 30, 1935 in Tupelo, Mississippi. Billy had three younger sisters and one younger brother. The family lived about one mile north of where the Presley family lived on North Green Street. Billy became friends with Elvis after Elvis started school at Milam. The Welch children and Elvis would ride the school bus to and from school each day. Faye told us that Elvis would ride his bicycle about one mile with his guitar to visit with Billy. They would go into the back room and close the door to practice their singing. Billy would sing harmony with Elvis at school and at home after school. Faye said that her family members were all singers; they would sit out on the front porch and sing together. That was the days before television. Faye remembered Elvis calling Billy and talking about a way they could make some money picking and selling wild plums. They also tried picking cotton at a farm south of Verona, Mississippi. This was probably on the farm sharecropped by Eddie and Lavelle Smith near the "White Spot" south of Verona. Eddie and Lavelle were Elvis's aunt and uncle. Tony Eugene and Carroll Jr. were two of their boys that would hang out with Elvis after both families moved to Memphis. The White Spot was an old beer joint located between Verona and Shannon. One day of picking cotton was all the boys wanted. Elvis calling Billy Welch could indicate that the Presley family may have had a telephone while living at 1010 North Green Street. Faye said that both boys liked to play practical jokes on each other. The two were involved in comic books and movies, and had become interested in a green parrot named **KiKi**. The bird was in the Children's Book "Island of Adventure" written by Enid Blyton. One day Elvis called Billy to tell him he had a parrot. Billy was very excited, and rushed over to Elvis's house on his bicycle to see the parrot. The parrot was just a painted chalk parrot like the ones given away as prizes at the fair. Faye remembers the girls picking at Elvis because he would wear his cap turned backwards. Elvis must have started the fad of wearing caps turned backwards.

After Elvis moved to Memphis, the Welch family saw him when he attended a gospel singing in East Tupelo. Billy and Elvis talked about old times, but it was already getting hard for Elvis to be seen out in public. Elvis assured Billy that he was the same old Elvis.

In the summer of 1950, the Welch home burned and the family moved to Beech Springs Road at what is today called Barns Crossing, north of Tupelo. One afternoon in the summer of 1955 or 1956 Faye was sitting in the living room when a pink Cadillac pulls up in the front yard and out steps Elvis. He knocked on the front door and asks if Billy was home. Elvis knew where the new home was located, because he had written letters to Billy. It is too bad that the family did not keep the letters. Billy was not at home, but Uncle George Tully and Billy's younger brother were home. The three stayed on the porch and talked for a while but Faye stayed inside the house.

We are sure that Billy Welch will have additional Elvis stories to tell about his friendship with Elvis.

Evelyn Riley was one of the girls in Elvis's homeroom at Milam Junior High School. Evelyn's uncle Walton Riley was married to Gladys Smith's sister, Retha Smith. Evelyn and Elvis had the same Aunt and Uncle but they were not related to each other. They already knew each other when Elvis started to school at Milam. When Elvis was in school at Milam, Evelyn, Jo Ann Wages, Mary Glenda Metcalfe, Billy Welch, Lando Lee, and Elvis would sit in the basement during the lunch hour and eat their sandwiches. Elvis would stand on a table in the corner of the room and play his guitar and sing. One song he sang was "Keep Your Cold Icy Fingers Off Of Me" Elvis would always wear overalls and usually a plaid shirt. One day Elvis came to school barefoot. He was a very shy and quiet person, but always had a big smile on his face. Some of the students would make fun of Elvis because of the way he dressed, and because he carried that guitar with him.

Retha Smith, sister of Gladys died in a house fire about 1941.

When Evelyn's children were small, she would take them to visit Elvis at his home. Elvis would send the children birthday cards, but in later years, they did not visit often. She still has the birthday cards. Evelyn said that Elvis was a great person, always helping anyone he could.

Loading Dock At L. P. McCarty And Sons   Vernon May Have Driven One Of These Trucks

In 1948, Vernon and Sales Presley are both working for L. P. McCarty and Sons Wholesale Grocery. Vernon has worked at this job for about five years. This was a long term of employment for Vernon. Brother Frank Smith, pastor of the Assembly of God Church in East Tupelo, was working in the warehouse at McCarty's at the same time. Mr. Marcus Posey of Verona remembers working with Vernon and Sales Presley at McCarty's Wholesale. Marcus started working in the computer department of McCarty's in 1947, and worked there for twenty years.

Marcus Posey was born on the Main Street of old Richmond on December 9, 1921. Marcus attended Plantersville High School and then served in the Army Air Corp in World War II. He was discharged in December of 1945. L. P. McCarty Wholesale was the first business in Tupelo to have a computer, and Marcus was in on the ground floor. When his grandmother Rosie Young Estes was in the Tupelo Hospital needing a rare type of blood, Marcus remembers Vernon and Sales donating blood to her. He remembered that Vernon smoked his cigarettes until they were very short and that he had to have a skin cancer removed from his lip. He said that Vernon would wear an old military style cap with a hard bill. Marcus is sure that Elvis would have visited Vernon or Brother Frank Smith at work, but he has no memory of Elvis. Marcus is the only person that remembered working with Vernon when he lived in Tupelo.

September of 1948 Elvis enrolled in the eighth grade at Milam Junior High School. Elvis was removed from school eight weeks into the semester, because the family moves to Memphis. We do not believe that Gladys would have been in any way happy about this move away from her friends and everything she was familiar with. She always wanted to return to her friends in East Tupelo. Vernon had left town many times to find work, but only once had he taken his family with him. He did not have a job waiting for him in Memphis. It would appear that Vernon did not intend to return to Tupelo, Mississippi. The reason for this move is not completely understood. The Tupelo story is that they moved to Memphis looking for a better life. How is Memphis a better life than Tupelo in 1948? Vernon may have been looking for an easier life, but he had no job waiting for him, and no place to live. They have no relatives living in Memphis at this time. Later, the entire Smith family and part of the Presley family follows them to Memphis. Vernon had worked at one job for about five years. This was the longest time Vernon worked at one job. Vernon had quit his job for some reason, or he had been fired from the job for some reason. It is never a good idea to quit one job before you have another one. There has been speculation that Vernon had to move from Tupelo to avoid going back to jail. Vernon may have been caught selling bootleg alcohol. The Smith and Presley families were both familiar with the use of alcohol. The quick move out of town would appear that Vernon was running from something. This was not Vernon's normal move to find work. The other times Vernon worked out of Tupelo, he would leave Gladys and Elvis at home. His selling everything and taking Gladys and Elvis with him is an indication that he did not plan to return to Tupelo.

I asked Marcus Posey if he remembered anything about Vernon's leaving L. P. McCarty and Sons. He did not remember anything about why Vernon left, but he did remember that L. P. McCarty did have a large amount of cigarettes stolen from the warehouse about that time. With Vernon having served time in prison, he may have been a suspect in the theft of the cigarettes. Vernon's early prison record would have been a handicap for him all of his life.

Billy Smith is a first cousin of Elvis who moved to

Memphis with the Presley family. Billy's father was Travis Smith, brother to Gladys. Travis Smith is the same man that served time in Parchman with Vernon because of selling the hog to Orville Bean in 1937. According to the book, Elvis Aaron Presley, Revelations from the Memphis Mafia, Billy Smith said, "my daddy said that he wasn't any better off than when he first got out of prison, because he was still sharecropping". He and Uncle Vernon thought if they moved to a bigger city, things would be better. Vernon said, "There's got to be more than this." So we ended up moving to Memphis, Vernon and Daddy had gone there together before. They stayed three weeks and couldn't find anything. This time, Daddy sold two cows and killed our hog to get some money, about $105. They had their cooked out lard and salted-down pork, and that money, which was enough to get by on until somebody got a job. I think Vernon sold something, too. I'm pretty sure we come in Daddy's car, a 1937 or 1939 green Plymouth. There were seven of us in that one car, Daddy and Mama, me and my older brother, Bobby, and Gladys, Vernon, and Elvis, and all of our belongings. This was about November of 1948. I was five years old, but I remember every dang mile."

The story as told by Billy Smith is somewhat different from Tupelo's story. The fact that Vernon and Travis planned this move might indicate that Vernon was not on the run. They did not have to slip off during the night, but Vernon did not have a future in Tupelo, Mississippi. For Travis to sell the cows and kill the hog would have taken some time. Elvis' eighth grade class gave him a going away party where he was allowed to sing to the class, which would indicate that they knew he was leaving.

We may never know all of reasons for the move, but initially they did not have a better life in Memphis. Gladys returned to East Tupelo every opportunity she had. This move was just another bad decision Vernon made for his little family, but later this decision would turn out to be pure gold.

The Presley family moved into a Rooming house at 370 Washington Street, Memphis, Tennessee. On November 8, 1948, Elvis enrolls in the eighth grade at Humes High School. The rest of this story has been well documented by other authors and researchers.

Gladys and Elvis In Memphis

The Roots of Elvis

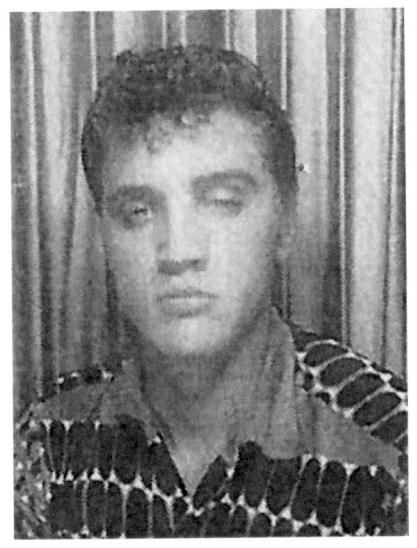

Elvis After Tupelo

Conclusion

Our search for the roots of Elvis Presley did not always lead us to the results that we expected. Because of the marketing of the entertainer Elvis, we had several misconceptions about Elvis the person. The Presley family is from and many still live in Itawamba County, Mississippi. Elvis was born in East Tupelo and lived there until he was three years old. The next five and one half years Elvis lived in the Mill Town area of South Tupelo. Elvis attended the first and second grade at the Ledyard School in South Tupelo. From the summer of 1943 until the summer of 1946, Elvis lived at various locations in East Tupelo. Elvis lived for a short time on the corner of Commerce and Main Street before moving to Mulberry Alley. Elvis never lived in the Shake Rag area of Tupelo, and Gladys would never have allowed Elvis to play there. Elvis family next moved to north Green Street, which was a black area of Tupelo, but is not Shake Rag.

Elvis was taught the words of the song "Old Shep" by his Pastor, Brother Frank Smith. Elvis was taught some different cords on the guitar by Brother Frank and other Elvis friends and relatives. Elvis did learn to play the piano while living on North Green Street. And he would visit the John Davis family because they owned a piano and Eugene Davis helped him learn to play.

Elvis did from an early age, have a strong desire to be a singer, and he would perform every chance that he got, even though he was very nervous when he was on stage. Elvis was blessed with a great voice that developed, as he grew older. Elvis's dream of being an entertainer was not to be a rock and roll star, because there was no such thing before Elvis. Elvis wanted to sing ballads and gospel music, and this is much of the music that he recorded. Elvis liked to attend movies, and he tried to emulate the movie stars and other local entertainers that he would watch. He liked to read comic books, and he would also try to imitate his favorite comic book heroes.

Elvis came from a very dysfunctional family. Neither parent had more that a sixth grade education. Vernon was not much of a father figure for a young Elvis. Vernon was gone from home much of the time that Elvis was a child, and he was not a very good provider for his family. Vernon's little family had to pack up and move many times. Gladys gave to Elvis all the love and devotion that she had to give. That is about all she had to give. Elvis always had many toys to play with, but his parents were not good money managers. The only advice his parents could give Elvis, was to get a good job as a truck driver and stay there. That is just what Elvis did after High School. Vernon's opinion was that he never knew a guitar player that ever made a nickel. This was not much encouragement, but that is all his parents knew.

We have interviewed people who were in school with Elvis and people who lived for a while next door to Elvis. Many of these people have no memories of Elvis as a child. Some have general memories of the schools and the times growing up around Tupelo, but few have specific memories of Elvis as a child. The two most recalled memories were Elvis singing 'Old Shep" at every opportunity, and his walking around Tupelo carrying his guitar. As a child, there was nothing special about

Elvis that would make him stand out from the other children, except his clothes and his carrying the guitar around. He was not one of the top students, he was not a great athlete, and he was not a leader in his class. He had a few good friends, but many of the kids picked on him about the way he dressed and him carrying his guitar around. He has been described as sweet, good, polite, sad, lonely, shy, bashful, and a mamma's boy. This is not the original image that I had of Elvis Presley, but I believe that this is the correct image of Elvis as a child.

After the family moved to Memphis, life did not change very much. Gladys, Vernon, and Elvis came back to Tupelo every chance they had. Elvis continued to go to the movies and to the local Gospel singings. He became friends with J. D. Sumner the base singer with the Stamps Quartet. J. D. Sumner said that Elvis started to wear his hair long because he wanted to look like J. D. Not until his junior year in high school do the students start to notice Elvis. That year Elvis starts to wear his hair longer than the other boys. Elvis had always dressed different from the other kids, but now his taste gets even wilder. These changes get him noticed more, but do not make him popular or accepted by the other students.

In 1951 Sun Studio recorded a song by Ike Turner and Jackie Brenston called "Rocket 88". The song was sold to Chess Records and was to become what many believe to be the first Rock and Roll song. Elvis would have listened to this song and to other Rhythm and Blues songs being recorded in Memphis, but his ambition was to sing gospel and ballads.

When Elvis walked into Sun Records, he did not have his own

developed style, he did not sound like anybody else, he did not have a band, he was not hanging out at clubs, he was not playing music anywhere, he was not a great guitar player, and he had not written any songs. Elvis Presley was like a blank canvas ready to be painted on, and Elvis the entertainer was created after he arrived at Sun Records. Many different people helped to paint the picture that would become Elvis Presley the entertainer.

As a child, Elvis did have a great desire to be an entertainer, and he did know the words to many songs. For a white boy in the early 1950's, Elvis dressed strange and looked strange. This made Elvis look like a rebel at a time the young people were looking for a rebel. The truth is that at this time Elvis had never been in any trouble, he did not drink or smoke, he did not run around with a gang or hang out in bars, he was very respectful of women, and he had not had sex. Any mother would have been proud of this son.

The movies "Rebel Without a Cause", "Thunder Road" and "Blackboard Jungle" were released in 1955. These movies contained bad boy characters that helped add to Elvis's image as a bad boy with his long hair and wild clothes. Elvis fit the image of the rebel young people were looking for.

There will never be, there can never be another Elvis Presley. Not because there are no good looking men with good voices, and not because there are no great songs, but because there can never be another time like the early 1950's. I am very fortunate to have grown up in that era.

Ikey Savery And James Ballard Breaking Ground For The Elvis Presley Youth Center In East Tupelo

Julian Riley, Rachel Ann Harden, And Mackey Hargett At The Tomb Of Rosella Presley In Itawamba County

The Roots of Elvis

1957